HIS MISTLETOE

MIRACLE

A Sugar Creek Novel

BY
JENNY B. JONES

PROLOGUE

F ROM HIS HARD bed on the concrete floor, Will Sinclair
heard his first sound of hope in four years.

A helicopter.

He raised himself to a sitting position, his eyes trying to
make sense of the darkness.

After all this time? Could they finally be coming for him?

His body ached with his wounds, and he hungered for food,
water, and freedom.

Yells in the Taliban language of *Pashto* echoed inside the
compound while shots erupted outside. A distant explosion
rocked the building, and Will instinctively ducked.

Limping, he shuffled the few feet to the door and stood
behind it, ready to fly if opened.

The chopper grew closer, and the sounds of attack ricocheted
in his ears. Will didn't know who had come to pounce on his
captors, but he wasn't afraid. The screams, the guns, none of it
could be any worse than the life he'd been living the last one-
thousand, four-hundred and sixty-seven days.

If death was coming for him, he welcomed it. He was ready.
He knew Heaven would be his destination.

Because Will had already lived through hell.

Seconds, minutes passed. There were no windows in this

prison of a room, no lights. The black of night was all he had, and it had long ago made his ears his best ally.

The thunderous sound of boots running down the hall had him backing up, his scarred body braced for whatever was on the other side of the door.

And then he heard it.

English.

"Left side clear!" a voice yelled.

"Right side clear," hollered another.

"Overhead clear. Go!"

He heard a grunt, then the door across from him busted open.

"Clear!"

Another door rattled on its hinges.

Will shifted away from the entrance until he was flat against the back wall.

The wooden door opened with a crash. The faint light from the hall seeped inside along with three men bearing guns and a swift urgency.

"Will Sinclair?"

He could've cried at the sound of his name. Instead all he could do was weakly nod as they asked more questions to prove his identity.

"Who are you?" Will finally asked.

"U.S. Special Forces." One man in black uniform assessed him through his night vision goggles. "Sir, we're here to take you home."

CHAPTER ONE

Eight Months Later

A SINCLAIR MAN knew how to charm a woman. It was in his smile. In his slow Southern lilt. In his obnoxiously beautiful DNA.

Will Sinclair was no exception.

But the former network reporter no longer had the clean-cut pretty boy face. His wavy blond hair had mysteriously darkened in captivity and was now longer than necessary, falling over his shirt collar. If you looked close enough, you might find a fleck or two of gray. Not that he cared. His face needed the attentions of a sharp razor and shaving cream. Four years in captivity changed a man. It could break you. At the very least, alter the heart.

But did it keep the ladies of Sugar Creek away?

No, it did not.

That was true today more than ever. He'd had a bad night of poker, too little sleep, and one soon-to-be former friend to thank for all of it.

Will had survived torture and imprisonment, but as his doorbell rang for the third time, he didn't know if he would survive this small Arkansas town. He stomped to the foyer, certain it would be someone of the female persuasion.

Will had barely finished his long-suffering sigh by the time he peeled open the door. "Good morning, Mrs. Beasley," he said to the woman smiling at his appearance. "You are a vision in that muumuu."

Shivering against the blistering December wind, the plump widow stood beside a porch post whose paint job had long expired. "My dear, I just stopped by to invite you to Christmas dinner. And to give you a taste of my cooking, I brought this coconut cream pie." She waved the baked good so close to his face, he nearly got a nose full of meringue. "Homemade crust."

Pie could make any man cave into temptation. "I bet this is your Blue Ribbon recipe, isn't it?" She blushed under his praise. "I'll just put it with . . . the rest."

"Do you know who else loves my pie?"

He didn't need a GPS to know where this was headed.

"My Alisha." Mrs. Beasley winked a brown eye. "You probably remember her from your childhood summers in Sugar Creek. She's all grown up now." She patted his bicep and gave an appreciative murmur. "Just like you."

"You tell her I said hello. And thank you for thinking of me. That's sure thoughtful of you. Now, if you'll excuse me, I have work—"

"Alisha would love to see you again. She moved back a few months ago." The gray-headed woman lowered her voice. "Nasty divorce. But not a bit of it was her fault."

"I'm sure it wasn't."

"We'd love to see you at our table. Give you two kids a chance to catch up on old times."

"I'm swamped with work, but thank you for the invitation." He'd been staring at the same chapter on his manuscript for days, but surely that still qualified as achievement. "So nice of you."

Peace and quiet. That's all Will wanted. He'd been here three months, and word had finally gotten out, despite his low profile. And regardless what his interfering family in South Carolina thought, he wasn't living like a mole. He'd shown his face in town maybe two or three times. Hung out at the diner with Noah, the town's mayor and his childhood friend. He was about to overdose on talking and civilities. Because, as he'd feared, the good folks of Sugar Creek now knew he was living there. And they were bent on smothering him with howdy-dos and casseroles.

"Thanks again, ma'am," Will said.

"I'll set a place for you at the table! And if you happen to hear of my Alisha coming off a gambling addiction, you do not pay that any mind."

"I know she's pure as an angel. Take care now."

And with that, he shut the door. Again.

After storing the pie in the refrigerator next to the banana pudding and a trifle, Will walked back down the hall to his office, a well-equipped and comfortable room in his vacation rental.

Wearing a gray Sugar Creek High School football t-shirt, dark jeans with his left knee peeking through, and no shoes, Will sat in his chair and propped his elbows on the burled walnut desk. Chapter seven was still just as blank as he'd left it when the doorbell rang the first time this morning. Just as blank as when he'd gone to bed last night. And just as blank as it had been this time last week.

He set his fingers to the keyboard. An old writing professor had once told him to just write, even if the words were nothing but junk. An empty page couldn't be edited.

Living as a hostage in the Middle East was a nightmare I thought I'd never have to face as a reporter or world traveler. The risk was always there, but you don't think it could happen to—

The doorbell gonged again, and Will lowered his head to his keyboard. What now?

He descended the stairs again, rubbing an old wound, and wondered if he should just move the desk to the front door.

"Hello, Will." Rachel Sands stood on his porch in a red dress and black stilettos, a combination that promised things dark and beautiful. "I was just passing through."

It was two o'clock on a Wednesday. Didn't anyone have a job in this town?

"What can I help you with, Miss Rachel?" Will forced himself not to take a step back as Rachel moved in, leaning a hip against his door frame. If she were a cat, she'd be purring and rubbing against his ankles.

"Word around town is you don't have anywhere to go for Christmas dinner."

This was his fifth invite of the day, and Will knew exactly who to blame for this outpouring of hospitality. His mother and whomever her insiders were. Donna Sinclair might be at her home in Charleston, but she had a network of friends all over the globe, and she'd surely enlisted them like soldiers to look after her wayward son.

"I have plenty of places I could be," Will said. "I am not a man without a spiral ham."

She laughed prettily and shook her blonde hair, the highlighted color a contrast to the lengthy, black lashes she batted now. "We all know what you're gonna do." She slinked one step closer, her perfume a hammer to his already aching head. "You're gonna spend every day like the others—locked inside this house, working away."

"Now that's not entirely true." His years reporting the news had never quite scrubbed his Southern drawl clean. "I'll also be watching sports and catching up on all the movies I've missed." Will attempted an amiable smile. "I do like to stay busy."

"I could help you with that."

In another life, he might've taken Rachel up on the offer. Now he felt tired even looking at her. "Your hospitality knows no bounds. You are too kind, Rachel." He glanced at his watch. "I'm sorry, I've got a conference call in five minutes. I need to—"

"Mayor Kincaid told me you needed some cheering up."

Ah, so that's who Will had to blame for today's parade of high-pressure sales.

Rachel clasped her hand on his. "My place. Seven o'clock, Christmas Eve." She gave his fingers a squeeze. "And I promise. . .dessert will be an indulgence you won't want to miss."

"I'll give that some thought. Now, I don't want to keep you. I know you have all that real estate to sell."

"Oh, I've always got time for—"

"Thanks for stopping by."

He shut the door right in her beauty pageant face and returned to his dusty office.

The worst part of captivity was the anger of surviving.
Somehow I had lived.
And twenty-three children had not.
The most brutal day of torture could not compare to the

thoughts, the visions in my own head.

Another knock from downstairs interrupted the slow clack of Will's keyboard. He shot from his chair. "For the love of—"

Favoring that right leg, he marched to the foyer like a man with blood on his mind. He wrenched open the door. "Look, sweetheart, if you're here to offer me a seat at your table for—"

"One night together, and we're already at the endearment stage?" Noah Kincaid took off his sunglasses and grinned.

"Get off my property, Mayor Kincaid." Will tried to shut the door, but Noah used his shoulder and nudged his way inside, bypassing Will and walking straight for the kitchen, as if he owned the place.

"Still a little sore about losing last night?" Noah reached into the stainless steel fridge and grabbed a water. "Your refrigerator's a disgrace. Do you eat anything besides peanut butter and hot dogs?"

"Yeah, a whole collection of desserts you're not welcome to. But after the day I've had, you really want to come in in here and disparage my Skippy?"

Noah's lips quirked, and he had the grace to look away.

"You got something to say?" Will asked.

"I say you need a freaking haircut and shave. You look like an intellectual grunge singer."

"This face got me three homemade pies by two o'clock. You know anything about that?"

"Doesn't sound familiar." Noah took a swig of water then smiled.

Will took a spoon to the center of the banana pudding. "Maybe if you can't handle losing a poker game, you shouldn't play."

"You cheated."

"How about you step closer and say that."

"You want to show me that deck of cards?"

"So to retaliate you tell every single girl and her mama that I'm desolate and alone for Christmas? This is the big bad revenge you said you were gonna get?"

"You say revenge." Noah sat down on the leather sofa with a piece of coconut cream pie. "I say it's just evidence of my caring heart. Plus, that's the price you pay for finally stepping out of your cave."

"You're gonna fix the mess you made, Noah" Will said. "I can't get a thing done with my door bell and phone ringing."

"You look like death," Noah said. "Your parents keep calling me wanting updates. They're worried sick."

"You know an upset family is the last thing I want, but I need some space."

"You should at least get out of the house more, so I can truthfully tell them you're not living like a hobbit."

"I did get out. And look where it got me—playing host to every single woman and her momma."

"Oh, the burden of being rich, famous, and an American hero."

Will's stomach burned with a familiar acid. He wasn't a hero. He was. . .Heck, he didn't know who he was anymore.

Noah picked at a piece of fuzz on the arm of the chair. "Will . . .sit down. I have some news I think you need to hear."

CHAPTER TWO

*B*AM! BAM! BAM!

Will startled at the noise outside, all conversation forgotten. A guy didn't survive a bomb blast and not have the occasional kickback.

Rising anger fueled his steps as he strode to the living room window and cast a frustrated gaze to the scene. It looked like Santa's elves had escaped to his lawn.

"What's all that?" Noah asked as he joined him.

"No idea." There were people in his yard. Uninvited people.

And, from the looks of it, they had Christmas on their minds.

Flinging open the front door, a shoeless Will crossed the cold yard and approached a burly man toting a ladder. "What's going on?"

The guy jerked a thumb behind him. "I'm just the hired help. Talk to the boss."

Will turned and found a honey-haired woman standing in the middle of his yard with her back toward the road, a clipboard in one hand, a coffee cup in the other, and if he wasn't mistaken, a giant snowman protruding from her top knot.

"More lights, Cecil!" she shouted.

Oh, no. Will was not having this.

He stalked her like a lion after a gazelle and tapped her on the shoulder. "Excuse me."

She turned, a smile on her face and a baby attached to her hip by some mummy-like contraption. "Hello."

"Hi?" He nearly took a step back as her piercing gaze met his. With her olive skin, chestnut eyes, and pink cotton-candy smile, she was one beautiful interloper. Will reminded himself he needed to get back to work, and he couldn't tolerate one more interruption. "Hi is all you have to say? You're disturbing the neighborhood, you're trespassing on this property, and you and your *Bring Your Baby to Work Day* are desecrating my space with Christmas junk."

She tucked the clipboard under her arm and wrapped her free hand around the stocking-capped baby. "Christmas *junk?*"

Will pinched the bridge of his nose and prayed for patience. "What are you doing, ma'am?"

"My name is Cordelia." She offered her hand to shake. "Cordelia Daring of Daring Displays."

"Nice to meet you." At least she hadn't recognized him yet and gone all starry-eyed and requested a selfie or a potholder for her casserole. "I repeat, what are you doing?"

"Decorating."

He tried not to focus on the glittery decoration in her hair or her holiday sweater that flashed red and green in lighted intervals. "Why?"

Cordelia Daring's smile took on a less hospitable tilt. "I thought I'd start a trend by decorating for the holiday." She crossed her fingers. "Sure hope it catches on."

An impertinent trespasser at that. "I mean, why right now,

right here?"

"Because I was feeding a baby and couldn't get here any earlier."

"Who authorized this?"

"The home owner."

On a tip from Noah, Will had leased the place online, having not so much as a phone call with the owner, Sylvie Sutton. Surely this was a rental violation of some sort. She couldn't dispatch a decorating crew to make his house look like the North Pole without at least a warning. "Can you just come back?"

"No," she said. "I can't." She jostled the baby and adjusted the cap over his ears to guard against the biting wind. "I have this crew for two hours and then—"

"Look, I'm trying to work," Will said.

"Oh, cool. Me too." Her brow lifted in a perfect arch of sarcasm. "So, how about you go back to your work, and I'll return to mine."

He dodged a man carrying an animatronic reindeer and bit back a curse. It was like he was stuck in a horrible made-for-TV Christmas movie. Where was the pause button? How did he change the channel?

"Miss Daring." Will softened his voice. As a former television journalist, he knew his husky timbre had defused many a sticky situation. "I'm here in Sugar Creek specifically for some peace and quiet."

"And you'll get it." That infuriating smile was back, dimpling her rosy cheeks and lighting her warm eyes. "As soon as the guys—"

"No, not in a few hours. I want quiet now." Forget tact and

sexy TV voice. "You need to leave."

Hearing that, she drew herself up tall. "We can't. If I don't finish this job then I don't—"

"I'm sorry." He called out to the crew. "Time to go home, fellas. No Christmas for this house, but thank you anyway."

"You can't send them away."

"I just did."

"You don't own the property." She consulted that blasted clipboard. "Mrs. Sutton does, and I have her explicit instructions to, and I quote, 'Make that place look like Christmas is a plague that devoured the house.'"

"Oh, it's definitely sick."

"The decorating continues."

Will had once loved the holidays. He hadn't always needed an Epi-Pen for the anaphylactic shock of good tidings and tinsel. But he wanted nothing to do with it this year. After returning to the states, he'd gone back to his home in Atlanta. He'd ignored his parents' many requests to return to Charleston for Sinclair gatherings. Even when they'd mailed him a plane ticket, he simply stuck it in a drawer and left for Arkansas. Sugar Creek had been a vacation spot for his family growing up, but there was no longer anything quaint or relaxing about the town now. His old friend Noah should've warned him Sugar Creek had morphed into the South's leading tourist spot for small-town Christmas. It was nauseating.

The baby began to kick his legs and cry. "Shhh, it's okay, Isaiah. The grumpy man didn't mean to scare you with his loud voice and Scroogey ways."

Good heavens, now she was using the baby in her tactics.

"You have five minutes to vacate the premises."

Cordelia pushed a gaudy star on her sweater, and it began to chime "Jingle Bells."

"I'm afraid you can't cancel Christmas," she said.

Will glared down at the psychotic elf. "You just watch me."

As if on cue his television movie took a horrible plot detour. A blue sedan crawled down the street, slowing as it neared his rent house, and a sick foreboding settled in the pit of Will's stomach. He didn't recognize that car, but it rolled toward them with an intention that he'd know anywhere. He saw the outline of hands wave from inside the vehicle as it confidently pulled into the driveway, the tires crunching over dead leaves and busted acorns.

"You've got to be kidding me." Will pressed two fingers to his throbbing temple as Cordelia's sweater changed tunes and the baby cried louder.

He'd been the recipient of a lot of visitors today. Each one more obnoxious than the next.

But these people arriving now?

They were next-level harassment.

A blight on his time and peace of mind.

Annoying wildflowers who showed up without invitation.

They. . .were his parents.

CHAPTER THREE

NOAH WALKED OUT the front door and zipped his down-filled coat. "So, yeah, about that thing I needed to tell you. . . ."

"Oh, no," Will heard himself say. This was not happening.

The decorator gal looked from Will to the car and back to Will. "Looks like you have another interruption."

She had no idea.

Car doors opened and his parents spilled out.

Cordelia Daring frowned and her eyes rounded as she got a better look at the couple approaching them. His parents were the Sinclairs—as in the hotel magnate Sinclairs. Known far and wide as much for their philanthropy as their empire and made even more famous by their three children.

"Oh, my gosh," Cordelia said on an awed whisper. "That's Donna and Marcus Sinclair. Their son is a Congressman and former pro football player. Their daughter dates some actor." She pivoted and faced Will. "Then that means you are . . . You were . . ."

He decided to help her out. "Will Sinclair."

"The television personality." She spoke in a trance-like state.

"Reporter," he corrected.

"The country thought you were dead. You were held hostage

for years."

He squirmed under her declarations. "Uh-huh. This is old news." The more pressing hot topic was his parents had just found him.

"Son!" His dad held out his still muscular open arms.

"Sweetheart!" Misty-eyed, his mother made a beeline for him, closing the distance and wrapping her son in her slender arms. "You have no idea how much I've missed you."

He was pretty sure he was going to hear all about it. "Good to see you, Mom."

"We've been a little worried." His dad patted him on the back before extracting Will from his mom's suffocating hug. "Hello, Noah. Good to see you again."

"Sir." Noah shook Marcus's hand, then hugged his grinning mom.

"What are you guys doing here?" Will asked.

"We came to see you," his dad said. "Your brother finally tracked you down through Noah. Didn't he tell you?"

Will leveled his friend with a stare of intimidation usually reserved for tight-lipped dictators. "No. He didn't."

"I was getting to it. Your twin offered me box seats for the Patriots, and one thing led to another."

Will's twin brother Alex had been as relentless as his folks in the phone calls and visits in the months after Will's rescue. With the holidays coming on, they'd amped up their efforts to the point that Will had just left town, needing time to work on his book in peace and quiet.

"I know you said you couldn't come to us for Christmas," Donna Sinclair said. "So we thought we'd bring Christmas to you. Isn't that wonderful?"

Wonderful would not have been the adjective he'd have chosen.

He noticed Cordelia Daring had ceased her moonstruck gaping and had returned to directing her league of elves.

"I thought we'd discussed I'm here in Sugar Creek to work." Will felt his frustration rise. "Are you just here for the day?" It was a laughable hope, but his family did love to travel.

His dad gave a hearty chuckle. "Your mom cooked up the best idea. We're all spending Christmas here—in Sugar Creek. We've never seen it in the winter. Isn't it great?"

"Great." Like a laptop battery, Will felt his energy reserves quickly depleting.

"We rented a house right on the creek a few miles from here," his mom said with way too much enthusiasm. "Your brother and sister-in-law are coming later, as well as your sister and her boyfriend. Won't it be amazing to all be together for the first Christmas in years?" His mother blinked back tears.

He couldn't help but be tired of seeing her cry in his presence. Naturally she'd cried when he'd been released and when his airplane landed on American soil. She'd cried when she'd seen his scars from the burns. The woman cried when she thought he wasn't looking. She thought Will didn't hear that all-too frequent catch in her voice or the way her eyes watered mid-conversation. Will knew he hadn't been a good son in the last eight months. But he was just trying to figure out how to be a human being again. And for that, he needed peace, quiet, and a significant reduction in the people he had to encounter.

"It will be like old times," his mom said. "Remember when

we used to come here when you were kids?"

Memory lane was closed for repairs. "It's good to see you." He slathered on an extra fib. "And I hope you can stay a few days, but like I've mentioned a few times, I'm not doing Christmas this year."

"You can't skip it entirely." His mother this with the same revulsion one reserved for stepping on slugs in bare feet or smelling spoiled meat.

"I'm swamped with work. I have a book that was due last week and a publisher breathing down my neck."

"Tell that publisher to breathe somewhere else," Donna Sinclair said. "That doesn't even sound sanitary."

Beside him, Noah bit his lip on a laugh. Lot of help he was.

Will continued his defense. "My agent's calling me every day, and I really need to get this project off my back." He'd yet to return to his old network, and he knew that worried his mom and dad as well.

His parents exchanged a mutual look of pity and concern.

He was so sick of that. How could he endure nearly two weeks of uncapped sympathy and *poor Will*?

"Well, hello there, Will Sinclair!"

All heads turned as two twenty-something neighbors waved from the street, pushing their sweater-wearing Chihuahuas in matching strollers.

Ellery and Sophie Cardman. He'd met them last week on a coffee run and noticed them walking in his neighborhood ever since. They looked fresh out of college and still dressed for an impromptu night at the club.

"My sister and I were just out walking our dogs," said Ellery with a giggle.

Donna Sinclair's eyes went to the sisters' shorts and matching cropped tank tops, barely covering their voluminous chests. It was quite the walking attire for a forty-degree day.

"Arkansas apparently makes women who are impervious to the elements," Donna muttered to her husband. "How fascinating. Honey, do we have any of that species in Charleston?"

Will's father wore a faint smile. "I surely wouldn't notice if we had."

"Hey, ladies." Will threw up a hand in greeting, his brain about to explode. He couldn't deal with one more thing here. "Mom, look, I have a deadline—"

The two women were not to be brushed off and steered their puppy wagons right to them.

"I want double lights in those trees!" Cordelia barked from the far yard. "Why is Mrs. Claus's head on the ground?"

Hadn't he sent that blinking lady on her way? Why was she still here? Why was anyone still here?

The Cardman sisters bounced and jostled until they joined their small group.

Will sent Noah a silent plea. *Help me.*

His friend nodded. *Under control.*

"Sophie and I were wondering if you'd like to come to our cocktail party tonight and—"

"He can't." Noah stepped beside Will. "Sorry, ladies, but our favorite Sugar Creek resident is regrettably unavailable."

Perky Sister Number One puckered her inflated bottom lip in a pout. "We have a hot tub."

"And he has a girlfriend," Noah blurted before doing a slow

rotation to face Will. "Yep, all locked down in a relationship."

His mother held a hand to her smiling mouth, ready to break into celebratory song. "You do? Who is this lucky lady?"

Noah searched the yard before zeroing in on his target. He pointed his finger toward the baby-carrying woman setting up luminaries along the driveway. "Cordelia Daring."

CHAPTER FOUR

"WHAT DO YOU mean they're not going to have Christmas?" Cordelia poured herself another cup of coffee, wondering if she'd relied on caffeine so much lately she was now like an addict immune to the charge.

"Steve Mason's doing the best he can." Her best friend Ananya checked a text on her ever-dinging phone. As a social worker, it seemed she was always on call. "He just took on three nephews and a niece he barely knows. He works long shifts at the airport and has no help from family. Give him a break."

Cordelia consulted the baby monitor on her coffee table as she sat on the couch, grateful to see six-month old Isaiah finally asleep. Her heart broke for him, the confusion and fear he must be feeling over the separation from his single mother during her incarceration, but what if his sleep-every-two-hour routine was just his thing? What if Cordelia never slept again? Thank God her job didn't involve brain surgery or operating heavy machinery.

"Cordelia, did you hear me?"

She tuned back into Ananya. "Steve Mason can't afford Christmas. Got it." With Ananya's supervision, Cordelia had taken a few bags of groceries over to Mr. Mason and the kids that afternoon, giving the siblings time with their baby brother.

"I'll see what I can do."

"We're working on some corporate and church donations," Ananya said, sipping her cocoa, "and the advocate volunteers always come through, but things are tight all over."

Cordelia had been Isaiah's foster mom for six weeks, four days, and ten hours. She felt like she'd slept about three minutes of that time, but it only took one look at her curly, black-haired Isaiah to know it was worth it. Fostering, Cordelia decided, was like skydiving. You were never really ready. You simply stepped out and did it, and somehow you often landed in exactly the right place.

When a sibling group of five had come into the foster care system, four had eventually gone to their bio uncle, while Isaiah, father unknown and clearly not related to the red-headed, fair-skinned Steve Mason, had been placed with Cordelia.

Ananya pushed the thick ropes of her dreadlocks away from her face. "You do this every year."

"What?"

"Adopt a handful of families for the holidays."

"It's kind of what the season is about."

"I know, but it's okay to take a year off. You have Isaiah and your business to think of. Speaking of business, have you decided if you're going back to the old job?"

Cordelia had taken a year leave of absence at the Fillmore and Associates accounting firm to turn her side hustle of Daring Displays into a full-time career. Her time was almost up, something her boss, Mr. Fillmore, reminded her almost daily, whether by phone or email. "I'm not sure."

"Cordelia, Isaiah's dad is out of the picture, and his mom's sentencing options aren't good. You need to be thinking about what you'll do if—"

"I know." She couldn't think about letting Isaiah go right now. "Let me focus on Christmas, okay?" Her smile returned as she thought of the movies still left to be watched, the adorable holiday jammies she'd bought for Isaiah for his pictures with Santa, and the Christmas party gifts she'd buy Isaiah and his siblings. The Mason family go without presents? Not on her watch.

"Leave the Masons' gifts to other people," Ananya said. "These things usually work out."

Cordelia didn't believe in leaving anything up to chance. Yes, her transmission suffered from seizures, and the tread on her Michelins was nearly gone. But she'd seen the sparse possessions of Steve Mason, the look of shock he wore still today in gaining guardianship of his brother's kids. She was struggling with one child, so she couldn't imagine suddenly taking on four. Steve's brother had overdosed last year, and his former sister-in-law was now in prison.

Ananya was the realist between the two of them, and she was right—Cordelia had no extra cash this year. After receiving a community grant, she'd opened her business, offering home staging, shop window displays, and seasonal decorating. She'd stepped away from her corporate accounting job onto the stairsteps of faith. She didn't know where those steps would lead, but so far it wasn't to a windfall of money.

With a stretch and a yawn, Ananya reached for a throw pillow. "What was it you'd wanted to tell me?"

"Oh, I met journalist Will Sinclair today."

Ananya sat upright, fatigue forgotten. "The guy from the news?"

"Yeah, he's here in Sugar Creek, renting a house to work on some book."

"You've got to be kidding me! Is he as handsome in person as he was on TV?"

Cordelia thought about his sky blue eyes and movie star hair in need of a cut. "He's okay."

"Just okay? Geez, you really are sleep-deprived."

She explained her odd encounter over the Christmas decorations. "I Googled him, and he's thirty-six. That's a little young to be yelling at people to get off your lawn." He was only six years older than she, but he'd regarded her with the eyes of someone who'd lived through lifetimes.

Ananya practically had cartoon hearts circling about her like a halo. "I can't imagine what he's been through. I bet he needs a good woman to help him heal, a shoulder to cry on, a hand to hold through—"

"Sorry to interrupt your fantasy, but Will Sinclair's a rude, arrogant jerk." A baby's cry from the opposite end of the house had Cordelia lifting her tired body from the couch and rising to her feet. "Be right back."

As she followed the sound of one unhappy baby, the doorbell rang.

"I'll get it," Ananya called.

"If it's Mrs. Burkowski, tell her I still don't want to buy one of her crocheted toilet bowl covers for my next job!" Cordelia entered the baby's dark nursery, the crib bathed in the soft glow of the nightlight. "Shh," she cooed as patted the mattress till she found his pacifier and plopped it back into his mouth. "You're okay, sweet boy," she whispered, running gentle fingers over his hair.

Like Steve Mason, Cordelia had very little family. Her father had passed away when she was a child, but her mother still lived in Sugar Creek. Not that they saw each other much. They were about as close as California to Florida. Paris to Sugar Creek. Maybe her lack of family had prompted Cordelia to finally follow through on her desire to give foster children a home. Isaiah was her third foster child and her first infant. Despite having read a handful of parenting books, she still felt like a caregiving flunkee. But as Cordelia watched Isaiah settle back to sleep, his little hands curled beneath his chin, his body at rest, she knew it was all worth it. For as long as this baby needed it, they would be each other's family.

Cordelia padded down the hall, her pajama pants swishing with each step. She returned to the living room only to find her best friend still standing at the front door. "Ananya, who is it?"

"Dreams do come true." Her wide-eyed friend swiveled toward Cordelia. "It's the rude, arrogant jerk."

CHAPTER FIVE

"HI." ANAYA'S SINGLE word came out in a wheezy breath. Will extended a hand. "I'm Will Sinclair."

"You sure are. I'm Anah-nah. I mean Namaya. I mean An-ya-ya." She shook her head, her dreadlocks like chimes around her face. "I don't really know who I am right now."

Cordelia needed to intervene before someone started drooling. "This is my friend *Ananya*." She was probably stupefied by the man's arrogance.

"It's nice to meet you." Will looked past her runway-gorgeous friend. "Cordelia, can I come in and talk to you?"

"Yes," Ananya said. "Yes, you can."

Cordelia held up a halting hand. "Not so fast. How did you find out where I live?"

"I was an investigative reporter," he said.

"Was?" Cordelia asked.

He didn't acknowledge her question. "I once found the FBI's third most wanted in a remote cave in Burma. Locating you was easy."

"He was looking for you," Ananya said dreamily. The cell phone in her pocket rang, and she took her eyes off Will only long enough to read the display. "Shoot. Duty calls. I need to go check on a family." She turned her love-drunk attention back to their guest. "I'm a social worker. I help children. I save lives and mend families. You know, in case that's something you're into. I could give you my number."

"Goodbye, Ananya." Cordelia gently pushed her out the door. "We'll talk about the Masons later."

At that reminder, her friend sobered. "Don't take on too much, Cordelia. Steve and the kids will be fine. The important thing is they have each other."

"Come on in." Cordelia stepped back and let Will inside, though she had no idea why he'd be at her house. "Did some of my workers leave their tools? Do you need help with the timer for the lights?"

"No. I think I can manage it." He stepped into her living room, his six-foot-something stature filling the narrow space.

Her house was small, but she'd decorated it with a mix of refurbished flea market and garage sale finds and the occasional new piece. Cordelia's latest furniture acquisition had been a crib.

Will made a study of her space, probably taking in her own ode to Christmas with the vintage aluminum tree, the white lights on the mantel, and the peppermint scent lightly emanating from a diffuser. He stooped over a side table to inspect a German nativity set she'd inherited from her great-grandmother.

"Is the baby asleep?" Will asked, breaking the stilted silence.

"Yes." For now. Until he woke up in a few hours to exercise his vocal chords and slam back another bottle.

"Noah tells me you're a single mom."

"Foster mom," she corrected, wondering where this was going. "Can I get you something to drink? A snack? A few minutes to work out whatever it is you're here to say?"

Will laughed quietly at that. "Noah also said you were quite the pistol."

"I'll take that as a compliment." Cordelia took a seat on the couch, very aware of her baggy pajama pants, pointy elf house shoes, and sugar plum fairy sweatshirt.

Will stood by the fireplace, warming his hands near the flame, but his attention remained fixed on her. "I have a proposition for you."

Oh, geez. "Is this one of those weird celebrity things? Whatever it is you're about to suggest, I'm probably not into it." Her eyes sparked with an idea. "Unless it's a drive through town to see all the lights or *It's a Wonderful Life* marathon?" From his sour face, she guessed Will Sinclair was not a kindred soul in her love of Christmas. "No?"

He settled on the brick hearth. "Not really my thing. In fact, this whole season is not my thing, and I'd like a little help with it."

Cordelia sprang to attention, hearing destiny's call for her display talents. "Tell me what you had in mind. Some automated light drips dangling from your trees? Perhaps carols piping from an outdoor speaker system? No, I know! What about—"

"I'd like you to be my girlfriend."

Her lips closed on her suggestion of a flocked front door. "What's that again? It almost sounded like you said—"

"I know it's weird, but I'd like you to pose as someone I'm dating."

Life was strange, wasn't it? Two years ago nobody could've told her she'd be decorating for others, raising other people's children, and getting a fake proposition from a man she'd regularly watched on television. "That's gonna be a definite no from me."

"Hear me out."

"Oh, yeah, because surely there's a logical explanation why a well-known, ridiculously handsome, stupidly rich man needs to ask humble Cordelia Daring to be his arm candy." She stood, fueled by bewilderment and indignity. "The bumper of my Ford's held on by camouflage duct tape and I have no idea what fork to use at fancy dinners!"

Will's full lips split into a grin. "You think I'm ridiculously handsome?"

"Can you focus here? I'm not your type. I'm the two-for-a-dollar taco type at the drive-thru." And on Tuesday nights, you bet that included free chips and salsa.

He leaned his elbows onto his knees, leveling her with that *let's talk serious issues* look she'd seen on his show. He was apparently too studly and divine for a coat and wore the sleeves of his Oxford shirt rolled to his forearms, like a weatherman forecasting impending doom. Except these forearms bore the webbed scars of a fire that had nearly taken his life. "Here's the deal, Miss Daring. I came to Sugar Creek to get some work done, away from the public eye and far from my family and friends. I have a book to finish, and I can't do that with my family buzzing around me like angry bees. You would be my excuse to get out of some holiday events."

"That's not all there is to this." She wagged a finger in his direction. "What aren't you telling me?"

He scrubbed a hand over his stubbled face. "Since my . . .rescue, I haven't seen a lot of my family."

"Why?"

"It doesn't matter."

"It does if we're joined at the heart."

Will looked like he was ready to take on their first fight. "Because they hover."

Cordelia thought of her mother, who appreciated her daughter more from a distance. "How could they be so cruel?"

"I hear that sass, but I need some space right now. I'm bombarded with calls, texts, visits. I came here to get some peace and quiet, and they think I'm two cups of eggnog away from climbing the water tower and leaping off."

"Are you?"

"No."

"That didn't sound completely convincing." She was pretty sure she saw an eye roll. "You want me to pretend to be your girlfriend so they'll think you have a life." A flit of a shadow traveled across his face, and she knew she'd hit her mark. "They think you're miserable, don't they?"

"It's simply a misunderstanding," Will said. "I need you to hang out with me at a few family gatherings so my family can go back to Charleston and know I'm fine. And so the ladies of Sugar Creek will let me walk to the coffee shop without bringing me baked goods or a blatant advance."

She clucked her tongue sympathetically. "You poor, abused man. The burden of being pretty and in demand. How will you carry on?"

Will was not amused. "I'll make this worth your while."

"Oh, let me guess. I get the honor and prestige of dangling from your famous arm?"

"No." He reached into the pocket of his jeans and produced a check. "For you."

Things suddenly weren't so entertaining anymore. "What is this?" Numbers were a strength, but Cordelia had to read the check amount three times. It was enough to pay off her last car repair bill and buy the Mason family a modest Christmas.

"That's the first half of your payment. I'll hand the second installment to you when my family packs up their caravan of crazy and heads out of town."

She swallowed hard, mentally depositing the money. "And when is that, did you say?"

"Christmas day."

Only twelve days, the check in her hand seemed to say. She could handle that.

No, she couldn't. This was insanity. "I don't think this is a good idea. Your family's never going to believe it."

"Funny story there," he said without humor. "They already do." He filled Cordelia in on Noah's fabrication.

"They can't seriously believe I'm your girlfriend?"

"After you left, Noah took it three steps further. Thanks to him, my family now thinks you'll get an engagement ring in your stocking and my last name for New Year's."

She couldn't help but laugh at the absurdity. "Why didn't you just correct him?

"I thought I could convince my folks to be on the next flight out, which was part of Noah's endgame. But those people aren't going anywhere. And my siblings are on the way in a few days."

"A big family gathering sounds nice." Why couldn't the man just appreciate he had a tribe of people who loved him?

"Cordelia, it's just for a few weeks. All you have to do is attend a handful of the planned events, concluding with a Christmas Eve dinner. You can invite your family, as well."

"No." She gripped the check. "That won't be necessary."

"We'll keep it strictly platonic. You have nothing to fear from me. I'm not going to make any advances toward you."

"You're right you're not."

"But we do have to make it look realistic. That's part of the deal."

"And what does that entail?" Was she nuts for even asking?

Will reached for a handful of red and green M&Ms in a nearby bowl and popped one in his mouth. "For starters, it'd be swell if you wouldn't look at me like you wanted to claw my face off."

"That sounds a bit extreme." She'd merely wanted to bash him over the head with a box of tinsel.

"For this to be believable we probably do need to have a Level One amount of physical contact."

"What's Level One?

His grin had probably set female viewers' hearts aflutter. "A little handholding, an arm around your shoulders. Rated G moves like that."

"I won't have to kiss you?"

"My dear Miss Daring, I've never had to pay anybody to kiss me." He rattled the candy in his hand like dice. "Though don't be surprised if you find yourself wanting to. Perfectly normal I hear."

Cordelia clamped her mouth shut before she said something she'd regret.

She thought of the money and all it would allow her to do. She could stock Steve Mason's refrigerator and pantry, buy the children presents, and think about a bigger, more reliable car for herself that would accommodate her new role as foster mother.

What was the worst that could happen?

"I accept your offer, Mr. Sinclair." The words surprised even her ears. "But the deal ends December twenty-fifth. I intend to use that money to help out Isaiah's siblings, so I'd advise you not to stiff me. Don't think I don't have enough hillbilly connections in these Ozark woods to seek out a little vigilante justice and make you go missing one more time."

"I'm a man of my word," he said. "Should we seal the agreement with a kiss?"

"I was thinking more a high five."

"A little unimaginative, but I can work with it." Will slapped her raised hand. "Your first assignment is to decorate the inside of my rent house. My parents informed me they're coming over for dinner before a mandatory trek to the lighting of the Christmas tree on the square this Friday."

Ideas and designs swooped into place in Cordelia's head. "I know just where to start. We'll need to go buy you some decorations."

Will's sigh could've blown snow off the rooftops. "I'll pick you up tomorrow at six."

She walked him to the door. "I'll be here with bells on."

He stepped onto her porch and gave her sugarplum fairy shirt one last grimace. "I hope you don't mean that literally."

CHAPTER SIX

WILL PICKED CORDELIA up at six on the dot.
She appreciated his punctuality, but would've preferred a little more time to change Isaiah's diaper and finish the rest of her panic attack.

What was she doing? How could she possibly convince anyone she was the girlfriend of this news celebrity? Cordelia was certainly no actress. In tenth grade, she'd auditioned for the lead in *Sound of Music* and gotten the role of Mute Nun Number Three.

Mute Nun Number One probably could've handled this, but not Cordelia.

"I think a tree is taking this too far."

These words greeted her as she answered the ring of her doorbell. He stood on her front porch, a stocking cap on his head that should've looked silly, but instead made him look like a calendar pinup for Mr. December. He wore a gray ski jacket that hinted at travel experience and a name brand that Cordelia would never be able to afford.

"If you want the interior of your house to look festive, you have to get a Christmas tree." Cordelia handed Will her diaper backpack, held a bundled Isaiah in her arms, and locked up her home.

"Trees are a stupid tradition."

"Maybe your Congressman brother can change that. Eliminate all Christmas tree frivolity. I'm sure it would make a solid platform for his reelection. But until you get the whole holiday banned, you're going to love the Wonderland Tree Farm."

"I doubt it."

The baby fussed in her arms. "Isaiah's offended by your seasonal cynicism."

"I'm pretty sure he was agreeing with me."

She held Isaiah close as they walked to Will's car, adjusting the thick blanket around the baby's head. "Pay no attention to anything you see or hear tonight," she whispered in Isaiah's little ear. "I promise it's for the greater good." Reaching into her coat pocket, she dug for her car keys and clicked twice.

"Are you already bailing on me?" Will stopped in the driveway.

"I need to get the car seat. It's kind of the legal thing to do."

"No need." Will's shaggy hair had been trimmed within reason at some point today, and he ran his fingers through his near-perfect tousled waves. "I bought one for Isaiah today."

She blinked, wondering if her snowflake earmuffs had garbled Will's words. "Did you say you bought a car seat?"

He held open the passenger car door. "That's what a man in a committed relationship does."

Oh, heavens.

He certainly knew how to impress.

"But maybe you could show me how to use the thing," Will said.

Still a little off balance, Cordelia could only nod.

While Cordelia secured the baby in the back, explaining as she went, Will stood close, leaning inside the car to see. They were inches apart, and so near she inhaled his cologne. Cordelia hadn't dated in a few years, so Will smelled like temptation and a big red danger sign. His proximity should've been uncomfortable—he was a stranger. Yet, it wasn't. She felt the wild impulse to lean against him, press her head to his chest and say, "Don't mind me, but I'm going to close my eyes for five minutes and imagine this is all real and everything in my life's going to be okay."

But she couldn't.

Because only crazy people did that.

"And that's how you buckle a baby in a car seat." Cordelia jumped back a little too suddenly, bumping into Will, who smacked his head against the door. "Oh, I'm sorry." She awkwardly patted his hair. Which felt very nice. Soft. How did he achieve that with no product? Why was he such a genetic wonder? "Very sorry."

He walked around to the driver's side. "You're not nervous are you, Cordelia?"

"Nope." She dove into the passenger seat, clutching the diaper backpack. "Not nervous at all. Let's go."

Will started the car, but made no move to throw it in drive.

She worked up a reassuring smile. "Here we go." She gestured to the road. "Look out, Sugar Creek. Fake Couple on the move."

"Are you sure you're okay?"

"Yep. Totally. Zen as a yogi master."

"Great. Then go ahead and shut your car door." He turned

the heat to max. "It might get a little drafty if you don't."

Oh, for heaven's sake.

Will made the rest of the drive surprisingly enjoyable. He was a big music fan with a wide range of genre preferences. They both liked 80s television reruns and classic spy movies. She argued Pierce Brosnan was an undervalued James Bond, while Will's devout loyalty to Connery couldn't be shaken or stirred. They stood on opposite ends politically, but had a lively debate on an issue Congress had newly addressed. Will admitted to being a voracious reader of nonfiction and historical tomes, while Cordelia invited him to her romance novel book club and preferred fluff over depressing, intellectual drags.

"Speaking of books," she said as he drove past a red and white blinking sign that declared they were near their destination. "How's your memoir coming along?"

His car hit a craterous pothole, nearly shooting her airborne. "It's fine."

"You're an award-winning journalist and *fine* is the word you're going with?"

The car turned down another dirt road. "The project could be better. The holidays are getting in the way of my writing time."

"Christmas isn't an inconvenience. It's magical and awe-inspiring and reverent and fun and—"

"You're the type who's playing holiday music in July."

"It's the sign of a sound mind and full heart."

Will parked next to a tree-laden SUV. "It's the sign of a mental imbalance."

She reached over and patted his shoulder. "Scrooge, the

Grinch, and Susan Lucci in the Lifetime movie classic *Miracle at Christmas* all saw the light and dropped their bah-hum-bug ways. I predict it might even happen to you."

"Your faith in me is uplifting." Will's smile fell flat. "And weird."

Cordelia rescued Isaiah from his carrier and walked toward the entrance. She turned a slow circle, taking big gulps of the pine-scented air, and hummed along to the festive music piped into hidden speakers. The Wonderland Tree Farm was a popular destination for families or really anyone with a pulse. Where else could you get such an authentic photo backdrop while eating a funnel cake and picking out the most perfect tree?

Will stopped by Harry's Holiday Hot Chocolate stand and ordered two deluxe mochas, extra whip. "Let me take the baby."

Cordelia hesitated.

"He's safe with me." Will gently plucked Isaiah from her hands. "Just drink your coffee and grab the first tree you see."

"That's not how you select one. It has to *feel* right." She walked down the first flawlessly symmetrical aisle of Douglas firs. "You need to look at the branches, touch the needles, envision the majestic tree in your home."

"I still think the one at the dollar store would've worked just as well."

Cordelia took a sip of her mocha, needing a caffeine infusion to deflect Will's dark vibes. "Just trust me."

They strolled past a five-person bluegrass band playing "Away in a Manger." The mandolin, guitar, and banjo wove together in holy harmony, giving Cordelia her first sense of peace of the night. And though the lead singer was a wee bit warbly, the song was imperfectly perfect, as bluegrass was meant to be. And, she decided, as Will's tree should be as well.

They continued on to the second row, and she watched Will work to keep Isaiah warm while he chatted to the baby as if Isaiah understood. And apparently he did, as her foster son repeatedly broke into gusty giggles. Why didn't he laugh that much with her? Wasn't she funny? Didn't she make silly faces and adorable sound effects? Why, yes she did. And then Will Sinclair just showed up, and he was an instant hit? Unacceptable.

"Why are you frowning?" Will asked. "We're in your happy place."

Cordelia took a deep breath, willing herself to blow out the negativity. "I stepped in sap."

"So let's discuss our story."

She nearly choked on her mocha. "We have a story?"

"If we want to be convincing to my family, we do."

"Great," she said. "Fabrication is a solid foundation for any relationship."

"Your foster mama has some sass." Will tickled Isaiah's chin. "How have I put up with her these two months?"

"You've been in Sugar Creek two months?"

"Three."

"How on earth have you kept that a secret till now?"

"Between restaurant delivery and Amazon, I don't have much need to get out."

"Don't you feel guilty for lying to your family about us?"

"No. I'm giving them the gift of peace of mind. Almost beats a gift certificate to Target."

"Oh, here's a good tree." She stopped at a Leyland Cypress.

"Nice round shape and—"

"Nah. Keep looking." Will was now blowing raspberries into Isaiah's neck, eliciting more giggles.

Look away from the hot man with shockingly good baby skills. Look away!

"So, how'd we meet?" he asked.

Cordelia let her hands drift over a branch, the foliage sliding across her fingers. "I rescued you from an ill-advised job as a dancing snowflake in the community Christmas pageant."

"I don't think so."

"You went door to door singing Holiday Grams?" She glanced back at Will. "You wore tights, of course."

He stopped at a Fraser Fir. "Isaiah, your foster mama was just checking out my legs."

"No, I wasn't!"

"I feel objectified." He caught up to Cordelia and nudged her shoulder. "But sometimes I appreciate a woman who boldly ogles."

"I wasn't—"

"Let's say we met at Noah and Emma's."

She'd sat in a few city council meetings with the mayor and his marketing director wife. "I barely know them."

"Which makes you extra grateful these new friends introduced you to the sexiest man you've ever met."

"Were you born with this arrogance or is it just something you're generously sharing for the holidays?"

Will lifted the baby higher against his chest. "Isaiah, Cordelia saw me across the room and it was love at first sight for her. Your foster mom's a little vain and into appearances, while I typically seek a deeper connection. I wanted to talk to her first and really get to know the heart and mind behind the woman."

She bit her lip, refusing to reward Will with a smile. "So Noah set us up?"

He nodded. "That works."

She pointed toward another tree. "That one is nice."

"Leans to the left."

She tilted her head and squinted, unable to see any such thing.

Will led them down another aisle. "We'll say we discovered we had so much in common, we've spent nearly every day together since."

"We've been dating three minutes, and you're already smothering me."

"It's not my fault you can't resist me. All our dating is probably why I can't get this book finished."

"Blaming me for your inadequacies." She lifted her cup to her lips. "We won't make it past New Year's."

"I promise not to cry when we break up."

"Noble." They turned a corner and walked side by side, the trees buffering the wind. "What are these things we have in common?"

"We both like me," Will said.

"Too unrealistic. Next."

"How do you feel about dogs?"

"Adore them. It's impossible to frown when you see a dog hanging out a car window."

"Book or movie?"

"Both."

"Agreed. Sports?"

"I can tolerate basketball."

"Now you like football," he said. "Don't forget my brother's a former NFL quarterback."

"Then I guess it's a good thing I'm not pretending to date him."

"He's married to a saint, and they're expecting baby number two this spring."

"Got it." Cordelia threw that in her mental file cabinet, trying to focus on the task at hand and not on the fact that she was so out of her league. Will was this rugged, model-gorgeous, award-winning journalist, with a twin brother who used to play pro ball, and if she remembered correctly, also looked like he'd taken a deep dive in the Beautiful People Gene Pool. Both had pedigree, money that probably did grow on trees, and what sounded like a caring, fully functional family. They had so little in common.

"What's your favorite food?" she asked as she stopped near a gorgeous fir.

"Cheap pizza."

She could respect that. "Mine's pasta."

"Red sauce or white?"

"Red is healthier."

"In other words, you like the white."

"So, so much."

He laughed at that and let Isaiah grab a branch.

"How tall's your ceiling?" Cordelia saw a tree that had her heart singing.

"Living room's probably ten feet."

She all but levitated to the evergreen, with its full branches, bright hue, and substantial stature. She could envision gold garland, vintage bubble lights, and a plaid tree skirt she'd spotted at a store downtown. "This is it," she declared.

"I don't—" Will clamped his lips on the rest of the sentence and pulled them both behind the tree.

Cordelia's nose pressed against his sweater. "I thought you agreed not to accost me during this fake relationship."

"Shhh." He jerked his chin toward the left while Isaiah babbled. "It's my neighbor, Mrs. Chen. Three o'clock."

"So?"

"So, she's here with her daughter, and twice when I've talked to Mrs. Chen she's used the term 'arranged marriage.'"

Cordelia knew Janet Chen from the bank, and the woman was harmless as her knitting needles. "I don't usually date someone easily scared by a five-foot-tall gal who likes cat sweaters, mall walks, and sings Sinatra karaoke every Tuesday at the Dixie Dairy."

"That short lady is lethal, and she's got a military-general strategy to get her daughter Mae married off quick."

"Maybe you should've picked Mae as your fake—"

"Mr. Sinclair! Oh, Will! Hello!"

He gave a low growl. "It's go time." And before Cordelia could say figgy pudding, Will reached for her hand, laced his fingers through hers, and gave her a resigned frown. "Don't forget you adore me."

CHAPTER SEVEN

"H ELLLOOO!" MRS. CHANG broke right between a family of five, her statuesque daughter behind her. "How delightful to run into you this evening!" The woman's eyes cut to their joined hands, but she soldiered on. "You can finally meet my daughter. Mae, this is Will Sinclair, famous television journalist and overall hero."

Cordelia felt Will tense at the description.

"It's an honor to meet you." Mae's smile was envious, with her full lips and not a smidge of lipstick on her teeth.

"Mae's a Dallas Cowboy cheerleader," Mrs. Chang said. "Did I tell you that?"

"Three times." Will wrapped an arm around Cordelia's shoulders and hauled her tight to his chest, right next to Isaiah. "Do you know Cordelia Daring?"

Mrs. Chang found a smile. "How are you, dear?"

Confused. Perplexed. Wondering why this man's embrace felt so unnervingly sweet. "Good, thank you. Nice night to pick a Christmas tree, isn't it?"

"It is," Mrs. Chang said, while her daughter seemed content to openly stare in appreciation at Will. "My daughter's in for Christmas break and wanted a tree for her room. Will, maybe you could help us carry it upstairs? You two could have so much to talk about with your traveling and football connections and such."

Subtle as a sledgehammer.

"I work some pretty long hours," Will said. "But I could probably round up some help and send it your way."

Not to be deterred, Mrs. Chang switched gears. "We're having dinner tomorrow night and would love to see you there. Wouldn't we, Mae?"

Mae nodded with an exuberant amount of enthusiasm, as if her mother had just said, *"Would you like to see Will take off his shirt?"*

"Thank you, ladies, but Cordelia's been begging me to get a tree, and I promised her we'd decorate it." He nudged his fake girlfriend in the ribs.

Cordelia slipped her gloved hand up his solid chest and rested her head near his shoulder. Her brain raced for convincing words, but there was no script to be found. "Um, yes. We're going to hang things and garland stuff and maybe drink eggnog, except I don't like egg drinks, and Will does, but he also likes cider, which is good too, and I like cider, and we'll probably cuddle like the cuddlers that we are because we're a couple. A real, true couple."

His hold on Cordelia tightened, as if he wanted to squeeze some assistance right into her.

"We should get our tree and go home," Will said. "Enjoy the rest of your evening, ladies." Will guided them away from the match-making mama and her pom-pom princess of a daughter.

"But that's the tree I wanted," Cordelia hissed.

"Just keep walking." He steered her down another aisle and

guided them toward the little cabin where an elf stood taking money. "Was that act the best you got, Daring?"

"I'm sorry." Her tone held little sincerity. "You said to pretend to be your girlfriend. You didn't say I needed to turn in an Oscar performance."

"I think Noah could've put in a more convincing portrayal of my significant other."

"And be more likely to kiss you."

Will stopped so suddenly, her hand slipped from his grip. As the night wind blew its icicled breath, Will closed the distance until there wasn't a snowflake's width between them. "You've mentioned kissing a few times."

"No, I haven't."

"Yeah." One brow raised. "You have. You thinking about it, Daring?"

"No." Maybe a few times, but that was completely normal. Wasn't it? It was *Will Sinclair*. Mrs. Claus herself would fantasize about a little lip lock after five minutes in his presence. "It never crossed my mind."

His head tilted to study her better, and a rogue's twinkle lit his eyes. "You haven't wondered at all?" He reached out and captured a strand of her long hair the breeze had freed, let his fingers run the wavy length of it, then slowly tucked it behind her ear, his gaze steady on hers. "Maybe we should practice."

She swallowed, as all thoughts of Christmas trees and cheerleaders cartwheeled away. "Practice?"

He nodded. "We do want to look convincing. You know, when we're cuddling like cuddlers."

"I . . . that is . . . you . . ."

"What if my family doesn't believe our ruse, and we have to get drastic?" Will sounded at least semi-serious. "If we have to throw them off with a kiss, do we really want it to be our first one?"

She couldn't move if the ground turned to ice.

Was he being serious?

Did she want him to be? Kissing practice wasn't the worst idea a man had thrown at her. It was better than running practice or tax prep practice.

Will's forehead creased. "I mean, I could go left, you go could right. Our noses might bump. The rhythm be all off, and you might not know where to put your hands."

Cordelia had a few ideas. "That. . .that sounds a bit complicated."

"Fake relationships often are." He traced the curve of her cheekbone with a cold finger.

As if drawn by a gravitational pull, she leaned toward him.

His eyes held hers, searing and searching. He slid his hand down her arm and tugged her toward him.

"Can we help you find a tree?"

Cordelia's head jerked at the arrival of two teenage helpers in matching Wonderland Tree Farm sweatshirts.

She took a healthy step away from Will as if he'd turned leprous. "No! No, thank you. Found our tree. It's a good one. Just spending quality time with my boyfriend here. We're super dating. This is a date. Will's my sweetie. We like trees."

From the droll look on Will's face, she knew she'd done it again. This pretending stuff was hard. Maybe she could *pretend* not to speak English.

"Check out is up ahead," a spiky-haired boy said. "We'll be glad to take care of you."

"Thank you," Will said, calm as a spring morning. As if he hadn't been about to kiss her.

Meanwhile her cheeks burned scorching hot, her heartbeat could surely be spotted thudding against her three layers of clothes, and her deodorant had surrendered and gone home. "Let's get out of here." Fueled by embarrassment, Cordelia's feet propelled her to the checkout, where, Saint Nicholas be praised, there was no waiting. "Mr. Sinclair will take the tree number seven on aisle three, row nine. And I'd like the small fir from row one as well."

Will caught up to her, and her anxious eyes automatically went to the baby, who was still cozy in his coat and passed out, oblivious to the elements and strain around him.

Cordelia handed cash to the high school girl using her cellphone to calculate payment. "I'd like the small tree taken to the Smithfield trailer park on Whitney Mountain. Is that too far for delivery?"

The girl nodded. "In town deliveries only."

She handed the gum-popping checker another twenty. "Does this put it in city limits?"

"We'll see it gets there."

"Who's that for?" Will asked.

"Some friends."

He frowned as two workers set off to aisle three, row nine. "Did I decide on a winner?"

"You did," Cordelia said.

"I'm pretty sure I rejected every one of them."

"I don't have time for you to work through your evergreen commitment issues."

He had the nerve to smile. "Do you have *time* to decorate tomorrow before my parents arrive?"

She did. Her day was wide open after a few morning appointments. "I'll have to check my schedule."

"Cordelia!"

She dropped her wallet into her purse and smiled at the familiar face approaching. "Mr. Fillmore." Who knew the tree farm would be the social spot of the night? "Kind of late picking your tree, aren't you?"

The white-haired man, her boss for the last ten years, glanced between her and Will. "Been busy, you know. End of year can be brutal. My wife bought a tree from the mall, but those fake things don't even compare, do they?" As was his pattern, he didn't give but a second's space for a response he didn't require. "Cordelia, looking forward to seeing you at the Christmas party next Saturday."

"Yes, sir."

"Are you still thinking about my offer?"

Anxiety was a tangle of Christmas lights around her heart. "I am. I'll let you know."

The man stuck out a hand to Will and handed him a card. "Arthur Fillmore, of the accounting firm Fillmore and Associates."

"Will Sinclair."

If Mr. Fillmore recognized Will, he gave no indication. But her boss rarely had his nose out of his spreadsheets to know what the weather was, let alone identify a television personality. "This lady here is one of my best accountants."

"Is she now?"

"Indeed. Went on a sabbatical this year to do her artsy-craftsy stuff, and we've yet to recover." He looked more than a little pained. "But we'll get her back. I'm sure she'll do what's right."

Isaiah roused in Will's arms, and she watched as her adept date whispered to the baby and popped his dangling pacifier back into his mouth. "An accountant." Will sliced her a look. "I had no idea Cordelia wore so many hats."

"You'll have to bring this fellow here to our Christmas party," Mr. Fillmore said. "It's going to be memorable."

"Will probably can't make it." Cordelia didn't think the yearly event of watered down punch, gas station gag gifts, and Mr. Fillmore's forced Christmas carol sing-along necessarily qualified as memorable.

"I wouldn't miss it, *babe*."

She glared at the interfering charmer. "We better get Isaiah back home. Good to see you, Mr. Fillmore."

"You as well, Cordelia. We'll talk soon."

She shoved her hands inside her pockets as her boss walked away. "I'll take Isaiah so you can have a break."

Will patted the baby's back. "He fell back to sleep. But he and I were wondering about this accounting job. I thought you were a staging decorator."

Nothing like explaining your life choices to someone you'd known mere days. "I am. The car's to the left."

"I know where the car is, and you seem to have two jobs. This is intel I need, don't you think?"

"No, I don't think you need to know every single detail of my life just to stage a fake two-week relationship."

"I'm fake offended."

Two minutes ago she wanted to kiss the man. Now she'd rather he walk into a field of firs and never return. "I've worked for Mr. Fillmore since my junior year in college. I took a year off when I won an entrepreneurial grant to take Daring Displays to the next level. Will, if we don't go right now, Isaiah's going to start crying for a bottle."

He lowered his head toward the slumbering baby. "There's a story here, Isaiah. Later, we'll crack open a bottle of Similac and you can tell me all about it."

"Don't be so dramatic. Not everything's a sensational scoop."

They drove home, and for once Cordelia barely saw the festive lights through town. She didn't sing harmony to the Christmas music on the radio. And she didn't make a mental note to buy bread, milk, and diapers when the local meteorologist broke in and forecasted possible snow and ice for next week. With her mind on a man who almost kissed her and a boss who dangled a well-paying job, Cordelia robotically plucked a sleeping Isaiah from his car seat when they arrived and walked herself to the door. It wasn't till she fumbled in her purse for her house keys that she realized Will had followed.

"Let me help." He reached for her purse. "May I?"

She released an uneven breath and gave a nod.

"Here we go." Will retrieved her keys in no time and unlocked the door.

"Good night." She stepped inside.

"Cordelia?"

She dropped the diaper bag to the floor and turned around. "Yes?"

"I had a good time tonight." He sounded reluctantly surprised.

"I did too."

"I'll see you tomorrow?"

She could almost see the gray flecks in those blue eyes. "Bright and early."

Will stepped off the porch. "One more thing."

Cordelia's hand stilled on the doorknob. "Yes?"

"Is a tux okay for your company Christmas party?"

She shut the door. Flicked off the porch light.

Put the baby to bed.

Then sat down with a gallon of cookie dough ice cream.

And one extra large spoon.

CHAPTER EIGHT

G RAY SKIES AND a leaning tower of boxes greeted Will when he opened his front door the next morning.

He was pretty sure there was a woman under there somewhere. "Are you here to help decorate or move in?"

Cordelia peeked around the stack as she shoved some of the boxes into his arms. "This is just one load. I barely had a peephole in my car to see to get here"

"I'm betting you thought it was worth the danger." He followed her outside, the wind cutting through his t-shirt and jeans, his uniform for most writing days.

Five trips later, his living room looked like a UPS warehouse.

"And you're going to get this done by this evening?" He didn't bother hiding the doubt in his voice. "My parents will be here at six."

"Then I guess you'd better let me get to work," Cordelia said.

"Where's Isaiah?" Will felt an unexpected stab of disappointment that she hadn't brought the baby. Not that it would've made any sense. He couldn't write a book and play with the baby at the same time. But he could've tried.

"The baby's at daycare." Cordelia peeled off her red coat, revealing a gingerbread sweatshirt, glittery skinny jeans, and giant snowflakes dangling from her ears. "He got tired of me making him decorate all the low branches."

"Is there anything you need? Besides a call to the fashion police?"

Ignoring that, she turned a half circle assessing the room, and giving him a better chance to study her. Her forehead scrunched in concentration, Cordelia wore little makeup, but he didn't think she needed it. In the news business, he was used to seeing women with mortician layers of makeup for the cameras, but he liked the face he was looking at so much better. Her hair was gathered high in a ponytail that seemed to bob and sway with an energy equal to its owner. Will wasn't sure, but he thought he saw a glimpse of some red glitter sprinkled about in her bangs, as if she had taken a walk through Santa's workshop before arriving.

This line of thought was going nowhere productive. Will needed to get his mind off his elfin fake girlfriend and focus on something else. Something besides her chewing on her lip as she measured his mantel. Or the way she smiled as she unwrapped an ornament in her hands, as if it held a secret only she knew. Then there was her method of—

Will shook his head and dislodged any more Cordelia thoughts. They were a brief diversion. And that was it.

Curious, he dug through a stack of boxes, found a star tree topper, and set it down on the coffee table. Next he rummaged through a bag and found a spool of tinsel big enough to wrap around the neighborhood.

"I thought you said the decorating was going to be all my job." Cordelia watched him over her shoulder as she began to wind greenery around his banister. "Remember, you told me to leave you alone so you could write your book in peace."

Will dropped a felt puppy ornament. "Of course. Yeah, I still mean it." He dusted off his jeans as he stood. "I'll be upstairs working, and I don't want to be bothered with any of this." The sight of his decorator's knowing smile followed him all the way up the wooden stairs where he sat back down at his computer and returned to his chapter ten.

He was just typing literature's most powerful opening sentence when the sound of Bing Crosby crooning drifted to his office.

Great.

Not only was he struggling for words today, but now he had to listen to Christmas carols? Hadn't he mentioned no excessive Christmas music in their deal? He'd certainly meant to.

Will's eyes returned to the laptop screen, and he proceeded to stare at it for the next hour. And if he tapped his foot along to the stupid music from downstairs, it was just a nervous tick. He added one more sentence to the chapter, then deleted it with aching regret. Everything he wrote was crap. He'd been in Sugar Creek three months to write, and he'd barely gained any ground. Will had written articles. He'd crafted copy for his news reports. Words were his thing. So why was this book like stabbing himself with an ice pick and writing with the blood?

Every time he sat down, his fingers poised over the keys, the sounds of the children laughing in the Durnama school came back to him, swirling in his consciousness, only to be followed by the horrific noises of the bomb and all that followed. There had been few survivors that day, and he didn't know why he'd been one. Some days the guilt was too much, the memories still too fresh, and the burn scars beneath his clothes, not nearly enough punishment to match the pain he carried in his heart. He saw the faces of the children when he closed his eyes at night; and when he woke up in the morning, the loss was almost too much to bear.

And yet his family wondered why he hadn't jumped back to work and wasn't quite up to weekly Sunday dinners. He hadn't told them all he'd seen and heard. All he'd endured during his imprisonment. No one else should have to live with those memories.

His holiday deejay downstairs switched to an up-tempo Mariah Carey ditty, and Will could hear Cordelia sing along. His lips curved in a smile when she tried to hit the high notes, and he imagined her down there stringing garlands and dancing around the Christmas tree. He picked up the pencil beside his laptop and let the eraser fall into percussion beats of the song.

A memory flitted across his mind, and he held it long enough to scribble it onto a notebook. Resistant to return to the harsh clack-clack of the keyboard, Will moved his hand across the page, making sweeping circles and strokes of letters that somehow formed words and sentences, and eventually paragraphs.

Forty-five minutes and eight pages of notes later, Will had more written than he'd managed in two weeks. He leaned back in his chair while the words to "Jingle Bell Rock" played a little too loudly. Somebody needed to tell that girl to turn down the music. A man couldn't work under these annoyingly festive conditions.

Making his way downstairs with an empty coffee cup, Will paused on the fifth step and watched his staging genius do her thing. Cordelia had wrapped her ponytail in a chaotic bun. She'd taken off her shoes and shimmied to the song belting from her phone as she wove a plaid ribbon around his tree. There was a cocoon of happiness around her, and it was all he could do to not go down there and beg her to let him in it.

This was a woman in her element. Garland made of greenery, pinecones, and antique sleigh bells coiled around his banister. Coordinating sprigs arched over his doorway, while a few burlap pillows reclined on his couch. The painting of children splashing in Beaver Lake that had hung over his mantel had been replaced with a quirky paint-by-number of people ice skating on a frozen pond. The painting was amateur at best, but somehow, wearing its proud white frame, it worked.

Cordelia stooped over a box and dug through tissue paper until she gently lifted a tray of tree decorations. Threading a gold ball with a hook, she reached up on tiptoe and aimed for a branch above her head.

Will eased down the stairs and joined her in the living room. "I can help you with that."

She made no effort to move as he came behind her, picked the dangling ball from her fingers, and held it high. "Right here?"

Cordelia turned her head and watched him. Her eyes briefly dipped to his mouth before jolting back to the tree. "To the left."

He wondered what was going through that mind of hers. "How about now?"

Cordelia shook her head and her hair rustled against his shirt. Will took one more step toward her, so close he could smell the vanilla notes of her perfume. See the graceful curve of her neck.

His arm brushed against her cheek as he settled the hook onto a branch then checked for her approval.

She turned in his arms, her toffee eyes holding his. "It's perfect."

Sometimes Will wondered if the bomb had rattled his common sense. He knew he should move. But he stepped even closer and reached out, his fingers threading her tendril of hair that had escaped. He let it slide across his hand, felt the texture against his skin before gently tucking it behind Cordelia's ear. Will had the wild feeling that if he put his mouth to hers, she just might reciprocate. Would her lips be as soft as they looked? Would Cordelia throw her whole heart into kissing him, just as she threw everything she had into Christmas? A speck of glitter on his cheek caught his eye, and he brushed it away as her eyes held his.

Somewhere a phone trilled loudly. The music stopped.

And the moment shattered like a fallen ornament.

Cordelia angled past him and reached for her phone. "I need to take this call." She stepped onto the porch and let the much-needed cold air rush inside to take her place.

Will rubbed his tired eyes and thought about banging his head against the trunk of the tree. He was in town to finish his book, and his alliance with Cordelia was simply to get his family off his back. To show them he was living, breathing, and functionally doing life.

He didn't have time for a holiday fling, and he sure didn't need to get involved with the poster child for holiday harassment.

So when Will stepped outside with his coat, he told himself it was just to make sure Cordelia was warm. Any man with manners would do the same. As she leaned against his porch post, he settled his jacket across her shoulders.

"Are you sure, Ananya?" she said, holding the phone tight to her ear. "But where does someone even get drugs in prison?" Her eyes closed and she nodded her head. "You know I'm a foster-only home. Adoption isn't an option for me right now. Yes, I'll keep it in mind. Thanks for the update." With a push of a button, the call was over, but Cordelia didn't move.

"It's kind of cold out here," Will said after a minute passed. His gaze roamed to the gray sky where clouds threatened to snow. He hadn't seen the white stuff in years. "Cordelia?" Without a care for any of their rules, he took her frigid hand in his. "Is everything okay?"

She stared blankly at their hands. "Isaiah's mom screwed up again. She hasn't even been sentenced yet."

The wind rattled the trees lining the street. "What does that mean?"

"The odds of her getting out of prison aren't good. And that means,"—She released a shaky exhale—"Isaiah and his siblings could soon be up for adoption."

CHAPTER NINE

"**D**O YOU WANT to talk about it?"

Cordelia sat on a barstool in Will's kitchen that night as he asked a question she'd already ignored a dozen times. "No."

"Have you thought about the possibility of adopting Isaiah?"

Her foster son was now in the capable hands of her neighbor for a few hours, which was probably for the best. Cordelia needed a little break to think, and the baby didn't need to be out in the cold two nights in a row. "I said I didn't want to get into it. Can I stress about one thing at a time? And why are you cooking your family dinner? Wouldn't it be easier to eat downtown?"

He tossed some garlic in a pan. "Because cooking was one of my things. I figure one meal from me will add some serious points to the tally my mom's keeping."

"What tally?"

"Donna Sinclair's 'Is he mentally stable or not' score card."

"They don't think you're crazy, Will."

"Maybe not, but they view any signs of a different me as cautionary." He added some butter. "So I want to put that to rest once and for all."

"How many times have you cooked since you've been

home?"

Will dug in the drawers until he found a large knife. "Twice."

Interesting. "So you cook, you hang out with your family, you celebrate the holidays, you—"

"Send them all back to Charleston and finish my book in peace."

And how long was Will staying in Sugar Creek? Did Cordelia even want to know? She'd spent the rest of the day decorating like a madwoman, working at turbo speeds with Will's all too frequent help. Maybe it had just been her overactive imagination, but she'd found him in her space quite a bit. His arm brushing against hers. Both of them reaching for an ornament at just the same time. His body close to hers as they inspected the final results.

Will checked the time on the stove clock. "Are you ready to be mobbed by my parents?"

Nerves fluttered like pine needles in her stomach. She pushed the thoughts of Isaiah away because tonight she was on stage for the performance of her ridiculous lifetime. Cordelia would have to convincingly pretend to be his girlfriend, and she still felt so unprepared. She knew little about Will. What she'd learned of his family had mostly come from an extensive internet search, and that only yielded information that intimidated her— like their massive wealth and accomplishments. The Sinclair family had hotels and resorts all over the world. And not the discount rate, free breakfast sort of accommodations.

Besides his successful career as a journalist, Will had quite the resume of philanthropic and charity work. The school that had been bombed had been his third one to open in Afghanistan. His brother Alex was now a big time congressman, and with his wife Lucy ran a handful of residence homes for kids who had aged out of the foster care system. Lucy traveled the country helping other organizations follow their model. And Will's sister Finley? Not only was she enviably gorgeous, the prodigy had graduated from a fancy music college and immediately gotten a job as a film score composer.

And then there was Cordelia. Who was she? An accountant. Who liked to decorate and blow up the holidays. She had a degree from a state college; she had a car that needed a hand crank to run, and her last philanthropic effort had been to drop a dollar in the jar at the gas station to go towards Billy Jo Jenkins' new liver.

"Cordelia." Will waved a spatula. "Hey, come back to me."

"I'm listening." She took a drink of her iced tea.

"I just said *Elf* was a terrible movie, and you didn't even flinch."

"I must've been deafened by your blasphemy."

He sliced into a loaf of French bread. "You're not nervous are you?"

There was no use in pretending otherwise. "What if we screw this up?

"Just have fun with it. We're not trying to convince them we're marriage material."

"You make it sound so easy."

"Maybe you complicate things."

"Says the man who can't communicate to his parents that he needs more time to decompress, so he hired a total stranger to pose as his girlfriend."

Grinning, Will poured olive oil into a bowl and threw in some seasonings. "Did I mention the house looks good?"

"Good?"

"Okay, incredible. I thought it would be fussy and overkill. But it's festive, yet masculine. Simple and. . .nice."

Nice.

Yet somehow the bland word felt like a compliment from Will's holiday-hating lips. Cordelia couldn't help but feel proud of her decorating feat. His vacation rental had gone from blah to more like a home for somebody who enjoyed his life, loved the people in it, and wanted to celebrate the season.

"Did you get much writing done today?" Cordelia asked.

"No."

The doorbell rang, and Cordelia nearly wet her pants. "They're early!" She leaped from the barstool. "I need to change. I've got glitter everywhere. Where's my makeup bag? Have you seen the bag with my clothes? My lucky bra's in there, and this night definitely calls for hairspray."

Cordelia zipped out of the kitchen and bolted down the hall, worried it was the nun tryouts all over again.

CHAPTER TEN

C ORDELIA TOOK ONE last look in the bathroom mirror and decided it would have to do. She'd forgotten mascara so she'd slathered on some lip gloss, brushed blush across her cheeks and eyelids, and prayed she was presentable.

The laughter grew louder as she tiptoed down the hall and into the living room. There sat Will and his parents. His mother perched right beside him on the couch, and Cordelia just knew he was itching to skooch over. His dad seemed to be mid-story and paused to laugh, a head-turning chuckle like Will's. The Sinclairs were some beautiful people with strong features. Mother and son shared the piercing blue eyes, while Will got his father's thick hair and strong jaw.

"There she is." Donna Sinclair caught sight of Cordelia hovering on the fringe and waved her toward them. "The wonderful decorator. Get on in here, Cordelia. I was just bragging on your work."

Will rose to his feet and met Cordelia halfway. As his eyes took in her candy cane sweater, his lips curved and he leaned close. "Does your sweater light up?" His whispered words tickled her ear.

"No."

"Cordelia . . ."

"Maybe just a few blinking lights. In ten rotating patterns." She tugged at the collar, which now seemed too tight. "But I turned off the sound because I wanted to keep it classy."

"I think it's perfect." He gave her an encouraging wink. "Just don't be too handsy. Try to control yourself around my mother."

"I heard that," Donna Sinclair said, moving to the adjacent love seat with her husband. "Stop pestering the girl and let her sit down. Cordelia, we're so glad you could join us tonight. Will's been telling us all about you."

"Has he?" Cordelia sank into the couch, lifting her backside when it came into contact with a displaced toy soldier ornament.

Will's hand inched toward hers as he sat beside her, and he gave her fingers a tug.

"Doesn't this house look beautiful, Marcus?" Donna asked.

Will's father nodded. "We pay big bucks to have our hotels trussed up half this good."

"I have Cordelia to thank for that," Will said. "She owns a staging business, and she's pretty famous in town. You'll see some of her work on the square."

How did Will know she'd decorated downtown?

After fifteen minutes of pleasantries that mostly included interview questions for Cordelia, they made their way to the kitchen.

"Smells divine." Donna Sinclair pulled out a chair at the breakfast nook. "You went to a lot of trouble, Will."

"What are we having?" his father asked. "All I've had today is fast food."

Will walked to the stove and stirred a large pot. "Fettuccine

Alfredo." His eyes found Cordelia's across the room. "White sauce is someone's favorite."

Two helpings and one brownie later, Cordelia sat in the front seat of Will's car as he drove the four of them toward the downtown square. The lighting of the tree had been delayed this year due to an electrical glitch with some suicidal squirrels, but better late than never. A few years ago the citizens of Sugar Creek had decided to make a name for themselves in the tourist industry, and with Mayor Noah Kincaid's help, the town was now on its way to being a must-see Christmas destination. The city had flourished with restaurants and B&Bs, and during the month leading to December 25th, visitors and residents could find daily and nightly holiday entertainment, from concerts to ice skating and tours of the Queen Anne style homes that dominated the older part of the town.

Will tapped his hands on the steering wheel, and Cordelia felt the tension emanate from him like a radioactive force-field. Pre-dinner conversation had been surface level at best. Things had gotten more personal over pasta, with Will skirting his parents' attempts at gleaning information from their son. The inquiries into his relationship with Cordelia were deftly handled, and thankfully didn't require Cordelia to go all Meryl Streep and convincingly step into her role. While Will grew slightly more glib and evasive as the meal wore on, Cordelia found herself unexpectedly enjoying the company of Donna and Marcus Sinclair. She thought they'd be snooty and dripping in diamonds and arrogance, but the couple was warm, entertaining, and shockingly down-to-earth. Donna still clipped coupons, and Marcus had driven the same truck since their daughter Finley had been born. Will acted as if their presence was a slight irritant, but didn't he hear the pride in his father's voice as he recounted childhood stories of mischievous little Sinclairs? And his mother could hardly eat her dinner for stealing glances at her son, love softening her gaze as she'd brush a crumb from his sleeve or plop another piece of bread on his plate.

"This house to the left is one of Cordelia's creations," Will said, pointing to a large, two-story historic home owned by the Wilson family. They'd given Cordelia complete artistic freedom, so she'd designed a toy workshop theme for the property, with a functioning assembly line and colors that defied tradition.

"Your displays are phenomenal," Donna said. "We really should talk to you about some of our hotels."

Marcus untied his scarf. "I'm all for it."

Cordelia double-checked her seatbelt because these compliments were liable to propel her to the moon. She was about to dramatically hyperventilate so convincingly, even Meryl couldn't heave air that skilled. Surely the Sinclairs were just being polite. Did they say off-handed things like this all the time? Cordelia had never been to a luxury hotel, let alone decorated anything close to one. She looked to Will for confirmation that his parents suffered from early-onset dementia, but his eyes were glued to the road.

"Cordelia, we're having dinner at our little rental cottage next Friday night," Donna said. "We'd love for you and Isaiah to join us."

"We might have plans." The windshield fogged, and Will turned on the defrost. "Cordelia has a thing."

"My thing got canceled." Cordelia patted Will's hand on the

armrest. "We'll bring dessert."

"Wonderful!" his mother said. "Have we mentioned how much we like her, Will?"

"At least a dozen times, Mom."

Will had hired Cordelia to help, and that's what she was going to do. Avoiding his family wasn't going to get them to leave him alone. It would only worry them more. They'd be headed back home to South Carolina in no time, and Will needed to take advantage of every opportunity to show them he was okay.

"Son, how's that book coming along?" his father asked from the backseat.

It was the second time the question had been tossed out, and Will finally answered. "Fine."

The tires whack-whacked along the pocked street.

The elder Mr. Sinclair wasn't deterred. "How long will the network hold your job?"

"Not sure. My leave's almost up."

"Are you going back?" his mother queried.

"Probably not."

"You were at the top of your game," Marcus said. "One of the best in your field."

"Yeah, until a bomb nearly took me out."

Cordelia wondered if she should run interference. "He's been working really hard on the memoir." She actually didn't know. Will said he hadn't gotten much done, but that didn't mean he hadn't put in the effort.

"You could manage our European properties," Marcus suggested. "I've got trouble in Paris, and I could use—"

"I'm not interested in the hotel business, Dad. I just need some time to figure things out. You don't have to worry about me moving back home and sleeping on your couch."

"You know you have a bedroom at our house anytime," Donna said. "I'd love for you to come stay for as long as you like."

But Will wasn't done with his father. "Things aren't the same. I can't just step out of a prison cell and put on my tie for the camera. I can't pretend that I can go back to how life was."

His mother leaned toward her son. "You take your time."

"I thought your book was coming out this spring," Marcus said. "The publisher sent photographers to our house last week to get some more pictures of the family. Didn't he do that months ago?"

"It's been pushed back."

"Good things are worth the wait." Cordelia unwrapped a peppermint, the cellophane loud as a fire engine in the cramped car.

"You can't heal if you pretend like everything's okay," Marcus said. "We just want to help."

Will turned the car a little too sharply to the left. "Duly noted. Now drop it."

A few minutes ticked by before Donna piped up once again. "Cordelia, dear, tell us about your family."

Oh, no.

Let's hop from one land mine to another.

Couldn't they discuss therapy options for Will? There was equine therapy, hot yoga, eating till you lost all respect for yourself. Or maybe they could revisit the idea of her handling some of their decor.

"Well." Cordelia searched for words that didn't make her sound pitiful and unworthy of a lobby renovation. "I'm an only child, and my mother lives in Sugar Creek. My dad passed away when I was a child."

"I'm so sorry," Donna said. "I know that must make the holidays hard."

"Not anymore," Cordelia said. "I adore every holiday."

Will turned down the heat. "She's got a whole sweater collection to prove it."

"What does your mother do?" Marcus asked.

Grateful for the dark of the car, Cordelia pushed past the old embarrassment. "She's an inventor."

"How wonderful," Donna said as her son parked the car, "Has she invented anything we might recognize?"

This part was always anticlimactic. "No, she's never really gotten anything off the ground." And rarely tried anymore.

"I'm sure your mother's excited to spend time with you at the holiday." Donna sighed happily. "Being with all three of my children and their loved ones is all I could ask for."

Cordelia said nothing and retreated into the silence like Will.

They walked the festively lit streets of the square, listening to the merry sounds of the high school orchestra. Giant snowflake lights hung overhead, Christmas trees blinked every few feet, and Santa Claus smiled for photos near the giant Douglas fir that he'd illuminate within the hour.

Donna stopped as a mule-pulled sleigh parked beside them. "I've read about those sleigh rides that take you to see lights and the decorated Victorian homes," she said. "Let's all jump in."

Will grabbed Cordelia's hand just as another sleigh arrived. "We'll take this one."

"But I thought we could all ride together," his mother said.

"Donna, let these two have some fun." Will's father slipped his arm around his wife. "You can keep me warm."

"At least take some of my homemade cocoa." His mother extracted a big thermos from her Mary Poppins purse. "One for each couple."

"Thanks," Will said with not nearly enough appreciation for melted, liquefied chocolate. He then helped Cordelia into the front sleigh, throwing a blanket over their legs as they sat down.

"One ride?" Cordelia shot a quick text to the babysitter to check on Isaiah. "Couldn't you have sucked it up for one single spin about town?"

Will exchanged a few niceties with the driver, then turned his attention to Cordelia. "I just spared you more of the Sinclair inquisition. You're welcome."

She glanced back at his parents in the sleigh behind them and waved. "They're watching us."

Will reeled Cordelia to him, tucking her beneath his arm. She closed her eyes for a few heartbeats, allowing herself the fantasy that Will was her boyfriend and this was the romantic night out. They were surrounded by carolers, lights, her decorated trees, and everything Cordelia loved about the most important holiday.

But Will wasn't her boyfriend, and at some point, he would finish that book and leave Sugar Creek. Cordelia was a means to an end for Will, and he was just a paycheck for her.

"Your family seems concerned about you," she said as they

turned onto Davis Street.

"Of course they are. That's why they're here. Since I've been back, my mom calls on average ten times a day. My dad texts and emails by the hour. My brother flies out to Atlanta to see me once a month. They send me self-help books, Bibles, prayers, articles in which I'm mentioned, inspirational memes from the internet."

"They care about you. They love you. I was expecting this overbearing, obnoxious family, and instead here's this mom and dad who are just trying to understand their son and help."

"I don't need their help."

"They seem to think you haven't dealt with what happened."

"What they think is that I should be over it by now. That I should forget it ever happened."

"That's not what I heard. I heard—"

"Believe me, that's what they mean. They don't understand why I'm not back on the news, back in the trenches, and living the life that I used to."

The air turned colder, and Cordelia pressed deeper into his side, drawing from his warmth. "Do you want your old life?"

"I want to be happy again." His hand idly played with hers. "I want to be able to sleep at night. But even my old life had something missing."

"Do you think the book can help you find it?"

"The book is a job. That's something I think you under-stand."

"What's that supposed to mean?"

"You worked as an accountant."

"And?"

"That's not what you want to do though, is it?"

She waited for the firm denial to hit her lips, but it just wouldn't come.

"That's what I thought," Will said.

"Accounting is much more reliable than the design and staging business. It's a good job."

"I've seen you work this week. Crunching numbers is not where your heart's at."

What did he know about her occupational choices? "I have a house payment, responsibilities, and a foster son. My accounting job makes sense. It's dependable and a steady paycheck with benefits. Decorating is something I could still do on the side." Though less so with foster children.

"Is that what you want?"

How had this gotten turned around on her? *He* was the one with the issues. "What I want is for you to hand me the cocoa."

The sleigh stopped to listen to a group of musicians singing "Deck the Halls."

"I'm sorry for tonight," Will said. "I think I used to be fun."

His eyes looked as storm-tossed as the dark clouds above them. "You've been through a lot, Will. The bombing, your capture, and imprisonment."

"Anytime I think about how bad things were I remember that I made it out alive. But because of me, so many of those kids didn't.

"They didn't die because of you. You can't blame yourself for that."

"The terrorists knew I was there. I was a famous person, from a famous family. A high-profile guy who didn't like to acknowledge that, so we had minimal security. So yeah, their death's on me. Families are broken because of me. Survivors are maimed because of my negligence. I pulled three kids from the wreckage, but couldn't save one more."

"You were there to help. Education radically changes lives and futures. Do you honestly think you could've stopped a terrorist?" She held his hand with a ferocity, wishing she could transfer truth right through her skin. "You have to know it wasn't your fault."

"I love your innocent outlook on things," Will said. "But about this, I'm afraid you're wrong."

CHAPTER ELEVEN

TWO NIGHTS LATER Will stood on Cordelia's front porch and rang the doorbell. The night air smelled of fireplace chimneys and a fool's errand.

What was he doing here? They'd ended their night at the square with an awkward, stilted goodbye, and he hadn't seen Cordelia since.

And he'd missed her. Her and that little squish of a baby.

Getting no response, Will knocked with his gloved fist, feeling like a nervous high schooler. And why? He was Will Sinclair. He had reported from battlefields and confronted evil dictators.

This was Cordelia.

Kind, compassionate Cordelia, who was one step away from having woodland creatures swarm her feet and cardinals light on her shoulder.

The door swung open and she held up a *wait a minute* finger, the phone to her ear. "I said I would stop by, and I will. Now go pick up that prescription the doctor ordered." She rolled her eyes as she bounced Isaiah on her hip. "Come in," she whispered and motioned Will inside. "Mom, I'll see you this week, and we'll look at your bank statement, okay? First National isn't out to get you, milk prices aren't highway robbery, and I'm mostly certain your new neighbor isn't a Russian spy.

I'm hanging up now. Love you." She punched a button, huffed out a breath, and pressed her head to Isaiah's. "My mom gets her passport stamped on the crazy train *way* too often."

"Join the club." His nerves dissolving, Will plucked the infant from Cordelia's arms and made his way to the living room.

"What are you doing here?"

"Isaiah, your foster mom loves our visits." Will hoisted the baby over his head and earned a belly laugh. "It's what keeps our relationship so smoking hot."

Cordelia's face relaxed into a reluctant smile.

He lifted the baby again, entranced with the kid's instant joy. "Sounds like I'm not the only one who has parental problems."

She watched Isaiah laugh, her expression one of captivated love. Will wanted to push pause and capture her face with a photo. The image would be better than any Mona Lisa. Cordelia loved that kid already, and when he left, it would tear her apart.

"My mom has moods," Cordelia said. "The holidays always cause flare ups, but nothing I can't handle. So . . .what are you doing here?"

It was then that he noticed Cordelia was dressed to go out-side. She wore a faire isle stocking cap, a coat fit for the Iditarod, and fuzzy boots that seemed to be eating the legs of her jeans. "Yeah . . .I was in the neighborhood."

"Were you?" It wasn't a question, but a doubtful charge.

He bounced Isaiah to his other shoulder. "Mapping out my route for caroling."

"Right. And who is it you'll be singing with?"

"It's a one-man show. Very exclusive. If you're nice to me, I might put you on the list for tambourine."

"Such incentive." Cordelia walked to him, brushed her hand over Isaiah's curly hair, and met Will's gaze. "Are you okay?"

No. He wasn't, but he wasn't sure why. And he sure as heck didn't know why his car had led him here. "My brother and family arrived this morning. The whole crew's going ice skating downtown tonight."

"That sounds fun."

"I told them I had a date with you."

Her hand stilled on Isaiah's head. "Why?

Will knew he sounded immature. "I've been with them all day, and I needed a break. I came here so—"

"So you wouldn't be totally lying?"

"Something like that." And because he wanted to see her, hear her laugh again. Will liked how the world wasn't so heavy when he was with her. The hundred thoughts playing percussion in his head seemed to quiet when Cordelia was near. He loved his family, but he felt battle-weary from the barrage of questions fired his way. A blob of drool plopped on his hand, bringing Will back to the present. "Isaiah, does your foster mommy have a big date tonight?" Not that the thought of her going out with some other guy bothered him. Not at all. Cordelia could see whomever she wanted to. It was a free country, and—

"It's actually Isaiah who has the date."

Relief filled Will's lungs. "Where to?"

"We're headed to Mitchell Crawford's ranch. He hosts a yearly Christmas party for area foster and low-income kids."

A flash of hesitation stilled his smile. "Sounds like an important night. I remember Crawford."

"Would you like to go? Seeing as how we're on a date to-night and all."

The phone in his pocket buzzed, and Will quickly checked the display. His sister. For the tenth time.

"Yes." Surely he could handle a party of kids. "I'll drive."

Will took them along the scenic route, driving by neighbor-hoods he knew would be glammed out in lights. Cordelia forced him to listen to Christmas music, unabashedly singing along as she pointed out the displays that had been her creation. Even in the dark of the car, he could see her whole face light up while she oooh'd and ahh'd as if she hadn't already seen all the decorations in town. While baby Isaiah babbled and cooed in the back seat, they drove over dirt roads that jostled and bumped. Farmhouses that had weathered generations stood in fields crunchy and barren from the arrival of winter. Finally, at Cordelia's direction, he turned down a lingering road that led them to one of Mitchell Crawford's giant barns, which, not surprisingly, was outlined in lights of every color.

"Did you design Crawford's setup?" Will turned off the car.

"I did. He gives me carte blanche, so his is always fun. It needs to be pretty, but very kid friendly."

It was a child's wonderland. Cordelia had really stepped up her game with this one, bringing in technology he had little concept of. There were three two-story animatronic Christmas trees that rotated through a laser light show in sync to popular music. Stringed lights formed a canopy overhead, like magical webs through the trees. Popular cartoon characters appeared in the sky like Bat signals. Wreaths bigger than semi-tires seemed to float midair, and in the distance sat a golden throne on a platform that surely was for the man of the hour, Santa himself.

Volunteers dressed as elves mixed and mingled through the crowd as Will, Cordelia, and Isaiah made their way through the throng of kids and families. Cordelia had the baby bundled in a marshmallowy coat and wind-blocking blanket, holding him close, while greeting people she knew.

"Isaiah! Isaiah!"

Cordelia turned and smiled at a small boy running ahead of his family. "Hey there, John Thomas." She squatted low, so the child with red hair and two missing front teeth could see the baby in her arms.

"Has he missed me?" the little boy asked.

"You bet he has. Haven't you, Isaiah?"

Isaiah stared at the kid, who couldn't be any older than five. Three more children soon joined them, followed by a man Will assumed to be the father.

"Hello, Miss Cordelia." The man wore a baseball cap, a quilted plaid jacket, and looked like he'd recently pulled an all-nighter.

"Hi, Steve. How are you guys? Are you ready to see Santa?"

The kids, ranging in ages from knee high to about ten jumped up and down, their red heads nodding, their cheeks and noses pink from the cold.

"You know all the food is free here, so be sure you get dinner and some snacks." Cordelia pointed to a pink trailer with a lighted bow on top big enough to illuminate space. "Miss Frannie's got some special cupcakes just for you tonight. She can't wait to see you."

The kids cast anxious gazes to their father. "You guys can go.

Max, you watch your brothers and sister. I'll be right there."

Cordelia didn't have long to wait before the kids were out of earshot. "The children look good, Steve. How are you doing?"

He shrugged. "My church is helping. We're making it." He glanced in the direction the kids had roamed. "They're great, but they're . . .a lot to handle."

"I'd love to bring dinner again soon."

"I've never taken help before in my life, Miss Cordelia. But right now a meal for us would just about make my week."

"Then I'll bring two. And dessert—but just for you. If you get those kids hyped up on sugar, they'll be even more to handle."

Steve gave a small laugh then shifted his focus to Isaiah. "And how's this big guy?"

"He's wonderful," Cordelia said. "Adjusting very well."

He nodded and chewed on his lip as if tasting regret. "We had a Christmas tree delivered to the house a few days ago. By chance do you know anything about that?"

Will recalled her ordering a tree for delivery, but Cordelia just shrugged. "Hope it was a good one."

"The kids went nuts." Steve's booted foot scuffed the ground. "Our case worker told me you wanted to bring presents out later."

"Ananya's helping me with the shopping lists," Cordelia said. "You can tell the kids it's from you and Santa."

He adjusted the bill of his Razorback ball cap. "Thank you, Cordelia. It means a lot." Steve turned his ear toward some sibling yelling in the distance. "I better go check on them. They've probably taken Miss Frannie hostage and eaten all her stock."

Steve left with haste, and Will felt the heavy shift in Cordelia's mood. "A fellow foster parent?"

"Yeah. Though not by choice." Her eyes skimmed the well-lit horizon. "Isaiah's mom had five kids. The oldest four were fathered by Steve's brother, who was a full time addict, in and out of prison in California. Sabra, the mom, is currently in jail awaiting a drug sentencing herself. Steve agreed to take guardianship of his brother's kids."

"That's a heavy load for one person."

"He's never had children. Doesn't have much family. He works long hours as an airplane mechanic, but I know he's struggling in every way."

Will nodded toward the direction the family had taken. "By chance is that one of the reasons you agreed to our deal?"

"Yes." Isaiah tugged Cordelia's scarf, and it fell to the ground.

Will retrieved the bright-colored thing and loosely wrapped it around her, steering clear of the baby. He lifted her hair, his fingers grazing the skin of her neck. "You're a good person, Cordelia Daring."

"Thank you. . ." Her long lashes brushed her cheeks as she watched his hands still holding the ends of her scarf. "You're not so bad yourself."

A kid in a flashing Santa hat bumped into Will, and he tensed. He felt sweat trickle down his back, despite the frigid temps. So many children here. The place was crawling with them.

"Will?"

Visions of other children flashed through his mind, squeezing his conscience until he had to take a step back and catch his breath.

"Hey, are you okay?" Cordelia shifted Isaiah and reached for Will's arm.

"Yeah. I'm fine." *Shake it off, man.* "It's nothing. Let's go find those cupcakes." And then he'd talk her into leaving.

"Will!" Noah Kincaid lifted a hand of greeting and began to walk their way. He dodged one teenager and nearly stepped on a toddler before finally joining them. "What a great party, huh?" The mayor slapped Will on the back and grinned at Cordelia. "How'd you get this guy out here?"

"He begged to tag along." Cordelia nudged Will with her shoulder. "Just can't get enough of Christmas."

"Is that right?" Noah planted his feet in a stance Will recognized as a precursor to a Kincaid sales pitch. "Will, we have a little situation with our Santa and need a last minute fill-in. What do you say?"

Will watched a school bus park and children spill out. "I say you're gonna make a great St. Nick."

"I intended to," Noah said, "but I just got a call about some busted pipes at city hall and need to meet the plumber."

"How about Mitchell Crawford?" Cordelia asked.

Noah shook his dark head. "The kids know him too well."

Will felt the noose of obligation tightening around his neck and tasted bitter shame on his tongue. Years ago he would've jumped at the chance to help out, but the thought of kids crawling all over him, their arms around him, telling him their hopes and wishes? It was a living nightmare. "I can't. I'm sorry."

"Are you sure?" Cordelia asked. "I think you'd look quite dashing in the costume. I can help you with the children."

"No." A bead of sweat tracked down his temple. It was irrational, illogical, but he couldn't breathe it away. "No Santa for me tonight."

Noah watched his friend with that blasted look of sympathy. "Okay, man. No worries. We'll catch up later." He clapped his hand on Will's shoulder. "Cordelia, good to see you."

She watched Noah disappear into the crowd then turned her attention back to Will. He waited for the questions, the lecture, the mention of "this is what your parents are talking about."

Instead Cordelia just smiled. "I'm proud of you for coming with me tonight." She reached out and straightened the collar of his coat, her hands smoothing across his chest. Her nearness was both a provocation and a comfort. "Would you like to leave now? Isaiah won't complain."

"Not necessary." He could push through a make it a little longer. Will put a hand to the curve of her waist and drew her closer, as if hoping to steal some of her sunlight. "But thank you."

"For what?"

He took a deep breath of the wintery, Ozark air. "For just being you."

CHAPTER TWELVE

"OH, CORDELIA! CORDELIA, dear! Yoo hoo!"

Cordelia stuck a bottle in Isaiah's mouth and watched a pair of friends walk her way. "Brace yourself," she said to Will. "Trouble and chaos are headed our direction."

"More kids?"

"No," she said. "Senior citizens."

They were soon joined by two women from Cordelia's book club. Sylvie Sutton, his landlord, sported a sassy pixie cut and elf ears while her best friend Frannie Nelson preened in a magenta wig.

"Hi, ladies," Cordelia said. "Frannie, I like your sweatshirt."

"Thank you. I made it myself." The woman held open her coat so they could get a better view of the holiday scene she'd created. Santa's googly eyes glowed as if suffering a demonic possession.

"Really captures the holiday," Will said.

Frannie and Sylvie made a thorough inspection and semi-silent analysis of him, not even bothering with finesse.

"How are you enjoying the house, Mr. Sinclair?" Sylvie asked.

He pulled his focus away from Frannie's sweatshirt, lest it hypnotize and bring him to the dark side. "It serves my purpose well."

"I hope you didn't mind my sending Cordelia over to decorate your yard."

"It was a surprise. But I've come to appreciate it."

"Nice to see you at our party," Frannie said. "And there's that cutie patootie Isaiah! Did you see his face light up when he saw me, Sylvie?"

"Probably gas," Sylvie said.

"We missed you at book club." Frannie pivoted to face Will. "But maybe you were otherwise occupied."

"I'm sorry I didn't show." Cordelia held back a grin. "I got caught up with work. It is my busiest month. But I did read the book."

Sylvie clapped her gloved hands. "Wasn't it amazing?"

"It was . . . something."

"It's a new Christmas classic for sure," Frannie said.

"What did you ladies read?" Will asked.

"*Snowed in with Santa's Sexy Son.*" Sylvie gave a low whistle.

"Sounds like it belongs right next to Dickens," Will said.

"A true family classic," Cordelia agreed. "Sylvie and Frannie are newly retired from the CIA. In an effort to find a hobby, they started a book club just for romance novels."

Will gave a polite nod of his head. "Thank you for your service to the country."

"Spreading the good news of kissing books certainly does benefit our great nation," Frannie said.

"I meant your time in the CIA."

"Oh, I suppose that helped too." Frannie patted the red streak in her funky locks. "Yeah, thanks."

"We are still available for on-the-spot security detail if you should feel threatened at any point tonight," Sylvie said.

Cordelia laughed. "You're not frisking Will tonight, ladies."

"We're big on safety." Frannie gave Will's bicep an unbidden squeeze. "But I think you might be okay."

Cordelia resituated Isaiah so he could see the two women making goo-goo eyes at him. "Frannie and Sylvie volunteer here every year."

Frannie gave the underside of Isaiah's chin a tickle with her glittery red nail. "We volunteer a lot, but even that can be dullsville. But not here at Crawford's ranch. We love this event and wouldn't miss it."

"Even if they did make us check our tasers at the door." Sylvie shrugged. "'Tis the season for rude demands."

Isaiah squealed and clapped his hands, inspiring a laugh from the group.

"We hear you, sweet baby." Frannie mimicked his hand-clapping. "You want your foster mama to go get me a funnel cake and coffee. Did I hear that right?"

Sylvie held up some cash. "He said two of each."

"Okay, okay." Cordelia shook her finger at the women. "But don't harass Will. At least not till I get back."

Sylvie chuckled as she watched Cordelia and Isaiah go. "Isn't that baby adorable?"

"He is," Will said.

"Adorable just like his foster mama." Frannie gave him hub-ba-hubba brows. "Am I right?"

Cordelia had stopped to talk to someone, and Will watched her hair blowing in the breeze. Her eyes were alight with the fanfare, completely jazzed to be in her element. Her pink lips opened in a laugh, and she touched the shoulder of the child she spoke to. Will had known what it meant to exist, yet not be alive. But Cordelia? She was life and passion and everything good.

His words came out scratchy and rough. "She's beautiful."

"I followed your story for years," Frannie said. "It's a miracle you're alive."

Miracle. It was a term that had been used around him a lot since he'd returned. "I guess it is."

"You guess?" Sylvie punched his arm with an impressive amount of heat. "Sugar, you're here for a reason. Believe that."

Will shifted his weight, suddenly uncomfortable under this strange scrutiny. It was as if these two could see inside his head. "Can I get you ladies some cocoa?"

"Nuh-uh." Frannie crossed her arms over her chest. "What you can get us are some answers, Mr. Hotsy Totsy Reporter."

"What are your intentions with Cordelia Daring?" Sylvie asked.

"I thought we'd just have a nice evening?"

"I think of her like my own granddaughter," Frannie said. "Except one that calls on my birthday and doesn't ask me for money."

"You won't find a sweeter gal in Sugar Creek." The blonde interrogator inspected the fingers of her leather glove. "One time a man broke my daughter's heart, and he was mysteriously relocated to a remote island in the Pacific."

These two might've had a unique collection of skills, but subtlety wasn't one of them. "I admire your concern for

Cordelia, but she and I are simply spending time together. Getting to know one another." That much was true. "We're not shopping for wedding china or picking out rings."

"Not yet," Sylvie said. "But if you do, I have a gold dealer in Switzerland who owes me a really big favor."

"The holidays stir up the romantic in all of us." Frannie's red lips lifted in a smile. "I personally get three times more hits on my profile on SouthernSingles.com in December. Of course, I also get three times more rejections, but I don't really find that relevant."

"It's the season of wonder and miracles." Sylvie widened her eyes for effect. "You might want to keep an eye out for things like that."

"I'll take that into consideration." Will was desperate to steer this conversation back to a safer topic. "This is an impressive event. So all the kids get toys?"

"Ridiculous transition, but yes," Sylvie said. "Toys and a new coat. Mitchell Crawford pours a lot into this community. Like Cordelia's grant."

"What grant?" Suddenly Will wasn't itching to leave the company of the CIA sisters just yet.

"Two years ago Mitchell started a grant program for young entrepreneurs," Sylvie said. "He awards it every November to an enterprising person under forty who'll operate a business that benefits the town. Out of 500 applicants, Cordelia was last year's winner."

"For Daring Displays?"

Frannie's hair swung as she nodded. "And she got it again just last month. That girl's on fire."

"Mitchell says she's yet to accept it." Sylvie watched him with eagle eyes. "The deadline is the day after Christmas. If Cordelia doesn't accept the grant, it goes to the runner-up. It's quite a bit of money. But I guess being her sweetie, you knew all that."

Blindfolded, these ladies could probably spot a liar from three counties away. "Actually I didn't. Why wouldn't Cordelia accept—"

"Why wouldn't I accept what?" Cordelia asked as she rejoined the group, Isaiah strapped to her chest in his wearable sling and a box of food in her hand.

"The prize for the most handsome date." Frannie slipped her arm through Will's. "This fellow here was just telling me how beautiful he thinks you are."

Cordelia laughed, sending a conspiratorial wink to Will. "Did he now? That's big praise coming from the most sought-after bachelor in Sugar Creek."

"But he's all yours." Sylvie grabbed the food. "Right, sweet potato?"

Will reached for Cordelia and pulled her close, pressing a kiss to the top of her head. "Anyone who knows Cordelia understands I'm the lucky one."

Frannie watched him for a few intimidating beats before giving Will a simple nod. And a look that said she'd cut him in his sleep. "I do believe you are, Will Sinclair. Now let me have this baby and give you two love birds a break."

After unhooking the complicated sling, Cordelia handed over Isaiah.

Frannie rained kisses all over his little face. "We'll go in the barn and look for Santa. That'll keep him warm."

Will watched the ladies walk away, feeling like he'd just survived a tornado—hanging on by a finger. "They're a little intense."

Cordelia snorted. "An undertow is intense. Those two are a tsunami."

"Miss Frannie mentioned something about a grant you won last year?"

Her hand paused in a wave to someone across the way. "Yes. It allowed me to take my sabbatical to see if I could make a full-time go of Daring Displays."

"Why haven't you claimed your grant for this year?"

"Wow." She crammed her hands in her coat pockets. "Sylvie and Frannie were full of information tonight."

"What are you waiting for, Cordelia?"

"It's not that easy. Just because I got it again doesn't mean quitting my accounting job and pursuing Daring Displays is the right thing to do. Not all of us were born wealthy."

His parents had been rich, but they'd made sure their kids weren't raised with enabling privilege. Will let that go for now. "You love staging and decorating. I saw your New Year's window display in the city library, and it looked like something out of an elite Manhattan store."

"Thank you. I love giving people a setting for their magical moments. Like this month, showing them what Christmas can look like, smell like, and feel like. It's about texture and color and lights." Her cheeks glowed and her animated hands moved with each word. "I want everyone to make memories with loved ones against a pretty backdrop. Instead of a lonely three-foot plastic tree that sits on your dining room table."

"Is that what you had growing up?"

Her eyes dimmed. "It was just an example."

Will doubted that. "Now tell me what you love about being an accountant?"

He could've sang the first stanza of "Jingle Bells" in the pause that followed.

"I like that my accounting job offers me a paycheck twice a month with benefits," she finally said as the wind whipped the tassel of her hat. "I suppose I enjoy how numbers are either right or wrong, and there's no gray area. I like fixing things for clients who can't see the problem."

"That sounds really good on paper, but when you talk about it, you're as shut down as a Christmas tree in January."

"In many traditions keeping the tree up past December is actually—"

"Is security what you want most out of life?" Will asked. She had too much talent to throw it all away.

"You don't know what it's like to be a single woman on your own. To be responsible for every aspect of your life. I value my independence, but it's hard. And I don't like lying awake at night wondering what I'm going to do if the washing machine goes out or if I need to buy new tires."

"And that's been your situation this year?"

"It's been successful, but—"

"But what? If you hadn't been successful, you wouldn't have gotten the grant again, right? Mr. Crawford doesn't just hand out money to any applicant with big dreams. He clearly thinks you have a solid plan and a good head on your shoulders. He saw enough profit and potential in your business. The question is, do you see it?"

His holiday enthusiast was shutting down quickly. "I appreciate your guidance counseling, but I feel very comfortable with my decisions. I haven't completely made up my mind to turn down the money and return to my old job, and I still have some time. I think about it every day. But it's my decision to make, and I'm tired of people butting in and telling me what to do." She turned and walked ahead of him. "I thought you of all people would understand."

CHAPTER THIRTEEN

Will Sinclair apparently got desperate when he didn't want to write.

For the third day since the event at Mitchell Crawford's, Will dropped by Cordelia's with no more notice than a text before leaving his house. Once, she'd had to madly grab newly washed bras hanging to dry and throw them in her dark closet. Another time, she'd missed his text, and he'd found her outside, tweaking her own light display and doing an impromptu dance to "All I Want For Christmas." All Cordelia *wanted* for Christmas was to get through a day with Will without embarrassing herself. She didn't have a lot of faith Santa could make that happen.

Cordelia snapped Isaiah into his car seat and watched Will's sedan ease into her drive. The baby babbled and kicked his little feet as if he knew.

"Yes, your favorite person is here." She handed Isaiah his new giraffe rattle. "But just remember who gets up with you in the middle of the night. I'd like to start seeing a little more loyalty out of you."

Will looked tired as he swung his long legs from the car and joined them. "No big projects today?"

The temperature had dropped ten degrees in the two hours

since lunch, and Cordelia wished she'd put on a coat. "I worked downtown this morning, then I've got a house staging later this afternoon."

"Where are you headed now?" he asked.

Cordelia noticed he wore the red scarf she'd given him yesterday, and it made her smile. She'd get him in a holiday sweater yet. "Dropping Isaiah off for a couple hours of daycare, then a quick stop by my mom's."

"Your mom's, huh? Need me to go and pose as your manny?"

"My last manny was a Latin bodybuilder, so I'm not sure she'd believe I've downgraded."

"Downgraded?" Will ran his hand over the duct tape holding Cordelia's bumper in place. "So maybe your last guy had six pack abs and pecs for days, but did Isaiah laugh at his barnyard impressions? I don't think so." Standing impossibly close to Cordelia, he peeked into the backseat to greet the baby. "Come on, let me go with you. I'm bored."

"How much have you written today?" she asked.

"I wrote a grocery list for the online delivery service."

"And?" He never wanted to talk about the book.

"And. . .that's all." Will straightened. "The muse is a fickle lady with punctuality issues. You should grab a coat. Storm's moving in."

There were already lots of jet stream currents right where Cordelia stood. She shut the door and took a step back, needing some space. "You don't want to visit my mom. She makes your muse look sweet and generous."

When a groaning gale of wind nearly pushed Cordelia over,

Will reached into his coat pocket, then pulled out a navy stocking cap. "It doesn't have glitter or high voltage flashy things, but this hat will help keep you warm." He eased it over her head, then let a hand slowly slide down her hair. His eyes held hers. "Better?"

Cordelia nodded, though she was anything but better. Nothing like getting turned on by men's outerwear. "Thanks. I'll return it when I get back."

"Come on, Cordelia." He braced a hand on the car and leaned toward her. "You've met my parents. Now it's time for me to meet yours. I promise not to tell your mom that you rarely eat vegetables and sometimes go outside with a wet head."

"You'd do anything to avoid working on that book, wouldn't you?"

"*Days of Our Lives* was a rerun, so you and my future mother-in-law are all I've got."

Oh, so now they were on their way to the fictional altar? Things sure moved fast in fake relationship world. "Fine. But I'm warning you—my mom's . . .eccentric."

"I like eccentric."

Will had no idea what he was in for. "Probably not her brand of it. She's grouchy, suspicious of everyone, and always thinks the sky's not only falling, but filled with toxic gasses planted by the government as part of their greater plan of mind control and world domination."

"She'll love me."

"I doubt it. But you hang on to that optimism."

CHAPTER FOURTEEN

THIS HAD BEEN a very bad idea.

After dropping the baby off at daycare, Cordelia reluctantly steered the car toward her mother's house while Will made entertaining chit-chat, none of which she heard. She was too busy running nightmare scenarios in her mind of the many ways her mother could humiliate her upon their arrival. It wasn't so much that her mother was mentally ill, but more that life had thrown Jane Daring a curveball long ago, and she'd spent every day since watering her bitterness like seeds in a victory garden.

As she turned down Persimmon Lane, Cordelia spotted the third house on the right, the one she grew up in, where her mother still lived. But now she assessed it as if seeing it for the first time. The home sat in a part of town dominated by 1970s Tudor ranch houses that had once worn their European Sunday best, but now appeared to favor the thrift shop discard pile. The lot did possess a few stately oak trees that stood tall and regal from decades of growth, stretching over the rooftops as if to see better things.

A one-eyed black cat hissed and scurried away as they walked to the door, arms laden with bags.

"Your brother?" Will asked as the cat hid in a nearby shrub and growled.

"One of the strays my mom feeds. While *she* often forgets to eat, she never fails to provide for her coven of homeless animals." Cordelia set her fist to the door and knocked. Most kids probably just walked into their parents' homes. But no, not her. She practically needed a TSA scan to make it past the mailbox. She knocked again. "Mom, it's me. Open up. It's freezing out here."

Click, click, click.

Cordelia set her teeth as she endured the familiar symphony of deadbolts and chains being set free.

Jane Daring finally opened the door, looking as if she'd lost a battle with a wind tunnel. Her chin-length gray hair was an unintentional salute to Albert Einstein, and her Bob Marley t-shirt hung wrinkled above paint-splattered jeans.

"Mom"—she took a deep breath, inhaling the scent of a bottled-up life—"this is Will."

"Good to meet you, Mrs. Daring." Will shook her hand, ever the gentleman.

"You look familiar." Her mother squinted. "You're that reporter that was kidnapped?"

"I am."

"Come back from the dead, did ya?"

"Okay." Cordelia was already done with this. "Just let us in before critical body parts go numb."

"I did come back from the dead," Will said behind her. "Some of our country's finest saved my life."

Her mother was easily ten inches shorter than Will, but still managed to look down her nose. "And so you naturally come to Sugar Creek, Arkansas. Who does that?"

"I heard it was the new hot spot," Will said with a gentle smile. "Between the double scoops at Dixie Dairy and Marv's Holstein Petting Zoo, it's easy to see why."

Her mom rolled her eyes, but finally allowed them admittance.

"Here's your dinner for this week." Cordelia set three shopping bags on her cluttered kitchen table. "We've got roast, chicken spaghetti, and tacos."

"You don't need to bring me food." Her mom followed her like an angry hen.

"I like you better when you're fed. Plus, the doctor seemed to think eating on a regular basis was a good idea."

"What do doctors know?"

Cordelia ignored that, no longer willing to argue with her mom's delusions of trust-busting grandeur. Instead, she grabbed a few of the dusty, dated magazines stacked on the table and shoved them under her sweater to throw away later.

Will sat down in a dining chair. All he needed was popcorn for the show.

"Did you go back to work yet?" her mother asked.

"I work every day." Cordelia stacked three plates in the sink with a little too much gusto.

"You know what I mean."

"Geez, Mom. Have you done the dishes at all this week?"

"Quit changing the topic."

"I got you enough paper plates to last a year. Why aren't you using those?"

"They're wasteful." Her mom hovered near her and frowned. "When do you go back to work full time?"

"After the holiday."

"So it's official?" Will asked.

"No." Why did she bring him again? "Not yet."

Jane grabbed a tea towel before it fell to the floor. "Get your head out of the clouds, Cordelia. So you had a good year with your frou-frou hobby. You honestly think you can continue making a living decorating Christmas trees and shop windows?"

"I now work with two of the top real estate agencies in the county." She felt heat climb up her neck. "Last week I got paid more for decorating a mansion on the golf course than I earned in a month at the firm."

"Because you don't ask for raises." Her mother shooed Cordelia away from the sink. "You need to let that boss know what you're worth. You're a numbers person. Throw him some numbers."

"Maybe I don't want to work with numbers anymore. I'm good at what I do."

Will smiled at Cordelia. "She really is."

"Nobody asked you," Jane swiveled her glare back to her daughter. "You saw what chasing lofty dreams did for our family."

Yes, there was truth to that. But her mom had lived with her enabling father and never had a head for business or the burden of responsibility until it was too late. "Just drop it. My job is my business."

Jane picked up a coffee cup and inspected the contents. "I'm a cautionary tale."

"You're a crabby woman who can't have a civil conversation anymore."

"I know what I'm talking about." Her mom slammed the mug on the table, stale coffee sloshing into a faint puddle. "You want to chase the wind, you go right ahead. But don't come crying to me when the money's gone, and you've lost it all." Her voice softened in the painful silence. "I know what that's like and . . . I don't want to see you go through what I did."

"I don't intend to." Cordelia pulled one final thing out of the bag, a red and green wrapped box and handed it to her mom. "I made you some cookies. They're your favorite." She kissed her mom's pale cheek. "I hope you have a good day—whether you want to or not. Let's go, Will."

Grabbing Will's coat sleeve, Cordelia stepped over a tower of newspapers and guided them out the front door, letting go as they hit the steps because the man simply wasn't moving fast enough. Not that there was any danger of her mom coming back after them like an angry pit bull. She would never bother to apologize or take back anything she ever said. It was always the same with her, and the holidays magnified it to an unbearable degree.

"Cordelia, wait." Will's long legs made quick work of catching up to her. He took her hand in his, unclenched her fingers, and extracted the car keys. "I'll drive."

She didn't even argue. Stomping to the passenger side, she got in and shut the door with a bang. Drawing on the five whole yoga classes she'd ever attended, Cordelia inhaled and held her breath for a count, then released in a whoosh.

It did nothing for her temper.

Will adjusted the seat, watching her with that reporter's scrutiny. "You okay over there?"

"I'm great. Wonderful. Who wouldn't be okay with such a loving, supportive mother?" She reached for her seatbelt, clicked it, then finally faced Will. "I told you it was going to be crazy. She's always needling, but I haven't let her get to me in a long time." Something she'd worked hard at overcoming. A silly source of pride.

Will maneuvered them out of the neighborhood. "Want me to stop at a bar? Maybe pop into the convenience store and get you a pack of cigs?"

His lame attempt at humor made her smile, then immediately tear up. The man had even switched the radio to Christmas music for her. Cordelia turned her head to the passenger window as her eyes pooled.

"Cordelia?"

She sniffed. "Hmm?"

Will slowed, then eased onto the shoulder, stopping right on Main Street. As cars whizzed by, he unbuckled, learned toward Cordelia, then pulled her into his arms. A fierce wind rocked the vehicle and sparse snowflakes peppered the windshield. But Cordelia only knew the warmth and comfort that was her fake boyfriend.

She breathed in the scent of him as her face pressed into his neck. "I'm fine," she mumbled. "I'll be fine."

"Okay." His hand rubbed her back, infusing her with small bits of calm. "Then be fine right here for a minute."

She was embarrassed, mad, upset. Now add to that: confused, light-headed, and wanting things she couldn't have.

His words came in a low rumble near her ear. "You're a good daughter, you know. How you handled yourself in there was higher-level adult skills."

She supposed a higher level would make the swan dive off even more spectacular. "My mom's a hot mess."

"There's one in every family."

But her mom was now her whole family.

Will slowly released her, then took both her hands in his. "Is she always that antagonistic?"

"It's not usually that dramatic. The holidays get to her."

"I take it she's not a fan of Christmas."

"Mom's pretty much against anything that might elicit happiness."

"You clearly didn't take after her in that regard."

"No, but according to her, *I'm* the misguided one."

"My journalistic instinct says there's a story here."

A five year old with working ears could pick up on that. Cordelia swiped at a stray tear that had the nerve to cling to her cheek. "My mom was an inventor—a dreamer, an idea woman. She was always coming up with something, always on the verge of a breakthrough she'd say. About the time a big corporation stole her prototype for a robotic trashcan, my dad got sick."

Will's thumb stroked across her hand. "I'm sorry. That had to be devastating."

"I was eight." And so far removed from the trauma. "He was gone by my ninth Christmas." The details sounded rusty on her tongue from years of keeping them to herself. "My dad had pretty much supported our family with his 'real' job of teaching, and when child services knocked on our door sometime later with complaints about my care, my mom was forced to go to work. Despite her PhD in quantum physics, she's worked as a janitor in a plant that makes staplers for nearly twenty years." Not that there was anything wrong with custodial work. But her mom had a degree that was nothing more than a forgotten piece of paper.

"Does she still invent things?" Will turned on her ancient seat warmers.

She had to appreciate a man who concerned himself with the temperature of her nether regions. "She tinkers occasionally, but she hasn't attempted a serious invention since she was robbed, as she says."

"That couldn't have been the most nurturing home to grow up in."

"I learned how to take care of myself—and her. I lived for the summers I'd spend with my grandma in Maine. Sometimes she'd fly me out for the holidays, knowing my mom would completely ignore them. Before my dad died, my mom went all out for Christmas. My dad loved it. He'd make her put trees in every room and mistletoe in every doorway."

"A man who encouraged kissing. I like him already."

"Suddenly being solely responsible for me and our finances was really hard for my mom. She didn't exactly transition easily into her role."

"So, because of that, she doesn't seem to condone your business venture."

"I try not to even discuss it with her because it always ends in a fight."

"That doesn't mean she's right."

"My mom has a lot of crazy notions—like government take-overs and corporate mind control, but sometimes she says something that's actually based in reality and common sense."

"I didn't hear anything resembling that today."

Said the kid born with a silver spoon in his mouth. "When you came back from Afghanistan, you didn't have to worry about a place to live, a car, a way to get back on your feet, did you?" It was a rhetorical question, and Will employed that big brain of his and chose not to respond. "If my business flopped, there would be no one to save me. I'd be living in my car and eating bologna sandwiches. You don't know what it's like to take a risk like this—to leave a good job and operate on a dream."

"You think I don't know risk? I just spent four years in a hole with terrorists who foiled my every attempt at escape. Before that I got death threats on a regular basis at the network. I opened a school in a zone littered with terrorists."

He didn't get it. "But did you ever worry if the network fired you, how you'd scrape up the rent?"

"No, but—"

"Then you couldn't possibly understand. Foster children are a priority for me, and I need to be able to provide for them beyond the monthly payment from the state. It's important I have stability and insurance and all of those things you take for granted."

"I don't take any of that for granted." The only heat in his expression was now one of temper. "I've got four networks calling me almost daily, and I don't even know that I can ever return to that life. I wake up every morning and have no clue what I want to be—if I should pick up where I left off or try something new. Whatever used to drive me to follow a good story isn't there anymore. My ability to craft an eloquent paragraph—gone. My passion for justice? Gone. I came home and all my assets had been sold and I had nothing. I had to start over in every way. So I know risk, Cordelia. Waking up for me some days was risk."

"That's not what I meant. I—"

"You got a grant last year that gave you an incredible opportunity, and you flourished—your business took off like crazy. I talked to Mitchell Crawford, and he said your profits tripled this year."

Any sympathy she had died a quick death. "You talked to Crawford about Daring Displays? What business is that of yours? What made you think for a second—"

"He doubled your grant amount for this year's award." Will grilled her like she was a crooked politician. "And you're not going to take it."

"I haven't made up my mind."

"I think you have." He jerked his head in the direction of her mom's. "Or that lady back there did it for you."

Who did this man think he was? "So I have one more year of the grant. What happens the year after that? And the one after that? I won't have that cushion of Crawford's money any longer."

"I saw the data you submitted to him. You don't even need his help now."

She sat in her seat with her mouth slack like a concussed cartoon character. "You had no right to look at my financials. Or my application to the grant."

Will didn't appear the least bit contrite. "Is it any of my business? No. But do you need someone to talk some sense into you? Yes."

This conversation was over. It was one thing to have to listen to guff from her mother, but to be lectured by a guy she'd known a week? No thanks.

Cordelia flung open the car door, letting the wicked wind swoop in and hopefully frost Will's know-it-all self. "Goodbye."

"Wait—"

She slammed the door and started walking, ignoring the waves of a few familiar folks shopping downtown.

The car crawled by her, window rolled down. "Get back in the car, Cordelia."

Grabbing the tail of her scarf, she threw it over her shoulder as she marched in the direction of her home. "Go butt into someone else's business, Sinclair."

"You tell 'em, honey!" An elderly woman called from a park bench.

"Hello, Mrs. Cooper," Cordelia called then continued to hotfoot it down the street.

"Would it help if I said I'm sorry?" Will asked, with his warm, cozy heat pouring out the window.

"No. Go away."

"This is nuts. You can be mad at me, but let me drive you home. You're gonna get pneumonia."

It sounded like a welcome alternative to spending one more second with him. With a perfect stop and pivot, she turned down Main Street and carried on, a soldier of independence, a champion for her right to privacy, a Shonda Rimes of Sugar Creek, taking control of her own life and destiny and—

Was that a new crepe food trailer?

No, soldier on, Cordelia!

Will drove the car at a snail's pace, following right by her side. "I'm sorry, Cordelia. Are you hearing me?"

"Pretty sure every soul in Benton County hears you!" hollered a nearby kid on a skateboard.

Cars piled up behind Will, and he waved them on. "I shouldn't have taken a peek at the documentation you sent Crawford," he called over the honk from a passing SUV. "I know a little about business, and I thought I'd help."

"I don't want your help."

"So you're just going to let your mom talk you out of your dream?"

She stopped and planted a hand on her hip. "My original childhood dream was to marry Prince Harry, develop a British accent, and own a lot of corgis. I accepted that wasn't going to work out, and maybe I can see the writing on the castle wall for this lofty goal as well."

"I'll buy a pack of corgis if you get in the car."

"I have to do this my way." Shonda Rimes would totally have brought a coat. "You don't understand."

"Maybe I don't," Will admitted as a tractor slammed on its brakes and gave him a one-fingered salute. "But I know when someone's running in the opposite way they should be going—and for all the wrong reasons."

Men! Rich, handsome, brooding men! "We're breaking up."

"What? No, we're not."

"Oh, yeah, we are." The words flew off her tongue, and there was no going back. "The deal's off." Lord, she was tired. Had she slept at all last night? All that was left of her was caffeine and rage.

"Tomorrow's a family dinner at my parents' place."

"Too bad for you."

Will drove onto the shoulder of the road. "How are you going to get money for the Mason family?"

"I'll figure it out."

"Cordelia, listen to me. You're being—"

She whirled on him then, pointing a finger in his infuriating, butinsky direction. "If you tell me I'm being irrational and overreacting, I *will* post your entire profile on Frannie's favorite dating site. I don't need your help with my business, and I don't need you meddling in my life." A fierce gale blew her scarf over her face, and she fought to dig herself out, completely giving up on any remnants of dignity. "And another thing! Maybe if you dealt with your own issues, you wouldn't be so invested in mine. Don't tell me to take a chance when you can't even handle a family dinner without a female security blanket."

"I'll be your security blanket, honey!" Mrs. Cooper yelled.

Cordelia cut into Walter Smith's manicured yard, admired his icicle lights, and disappeared behind the next house.

Leaving Will.

And a little piece of her heart.

CHAPTER FIFTEEN

THE BLUE BUNNY would fix everything.

Two days later, Cordelia piled groceries around Isaiah as he sat in his carrier in the middle of the shopping cart. "Do we want cookies and cream or caramel coffee crunch?" Isaiah sucked on his thumb and burped. "You're right." She grabbed the ice cream from the freezer. "We'll buy both."

Consulting the list on her phone, Cordelia pushed the cart to the next aisle. They needed baby formula again. And diapers. And maybe some brownies. Because if she dissolved into a mindless sugar coma, at least she wouldn't have to think about Will.

After their fight, he'd lit up her phone with calls and texts.

Until today, when her phone went eerily silent. Not even a telemarketer had called.

She had every right to tell him to mind his own business. Will had gone too far by getting her financial information from Mitchell Crawford. Okay, maybe she shouldn't have told him off in such a public and dramatic fashion. But there hadn't been any Christmas activities scheduled for the square that afternoon, so she'd done the town a service by providing some entertainment. They could've sold tickets. *Watch holiday sweater-wearing girl have a total meltdown as the grieving journalist drives by!*

Cordelia threw some lunchmeat in the cart and made her way to the bread aisle.

She normally wasn't one for hysterics, but she'd been so exhausted the day of their fight. Isaiah had woken her up three times the night before, and her brain had been jelly. Add to that, Mr. Fillmore had contacted her again, putting a little more force behind his nudge to return to work. This time he'd dangled an office with a window. People committed crimes and misdemeanors to get that kind of perk.

In another hour Will would be leaving to have dinner with his parents. All by himself. Without her.

He was a big boy. He could handle it, right?

Right!

She shoved her cart forward. And plowed into another shopper.

"Oh, I'm sorry."

The man turned around and recognition lit his face. "Cordelia?"

"Steve." She looked for Isaiah's siblings. "Didn't mean to bump into you. I guess I got distracted."

"I remember when I used to have ice cream for dinner." Longing filled Steve Mason's tired voice as he studied her grocery selections. "Now it's balanced meals, eat your veggies, don't hit your brother, and we don't eat spaghetti with our hands, John Thomas."

Cordelia laughed, not because it was funny, but because she understood. She knew what it was like to be that worn out and not know how to take care of these new small people in your home. To love being a parent, but miss the indulgences and freedoms of your old life. "Where are the kids tonight?"

"The church is having a foster-parents-night-out. I might've had them at the doors of the Sugar Creek Methodist before they even opened."

"It sounds like you deserve some ice cream too."

Steve reached in the cart and gave an interested Isaiah his finger to hold. "I'd planned to hang out with the guys and have a fun night out, but instead, I'm gonna go fold laundry and take a nap."

A nap. That sounded divine. "Time's a ticking. You better get to it."

"Yes, ma'am." Steve took two steps before turning back. "Thanks again for the presents you're getting the kids. I took them to see Santa yesterday, and they each had lengthy requests." He dug into his coat pocket. "I actually wrote some of them down—in case you want to see." He caught her hesitation. "But if not, that's okay. Whatever you have in mind will be much appreciated."

Cordelia blinked. "I'd love a list. Of course I would." She reached for the paper and felt it warm her palm.

"I was thinking maybe a Christmas morning delivery would be cool. Like Santa's stopped by."

Steve Mason had really been giving this some thought.

"Okay, then that's when I'll deliver the presents."

Growing bored, Isaiah let out a wail, and Cordelia scrambled in her bag for what was left of a bottle.

"I won't keep you anymore," Steve said. "But I wanted to thank you again. Your offer to help has been like a miracle."

FORTY-FIVE MINUTES AND one bowl of ice cream later, Cordelia stood on Will Sinclair's front porch, the moon shining overhead like a spotlight guiding her there.

He opened the door on her first knock, not bothering to hide the surprise on his face. "What are you doing here?"

"You have a family dinner tonight," she said.

"I'm all too aware." He stood there in the door, a paragon of tangy cologne and frustration. "But we broke up, remember? You tossed our love on the rocks and stomped all over it downtown while a giant inflatable Rudolph looked on."

Why wasn't he throwing himself at her feet in appreciation? "You were being a first class jerk. And Rudolph was definitely on my side."

"You jumped out of the car and walked down the street, shouting your dissatisfaction for all to hear."

"We have a large population of senior citizens in this town, so you can probably assume thirty percent of Sugar Creek totally missed it."

"What a comfort." His gaze roamed over her, taking in her candy cane sweater, matching earrings, and the ribbon that threaded through her braid. "You look beautiful, by the way. Almost like you're ready to come back to me and denounce your public rejection."

She bit her lip on a smile. "Are you going to invite me in?"

"Depends. Is there going to be more arguing?"

"Probably not."

"Pity," Will said. "I was kind of enjoying it."

Her heart lightened at that rakish grin, and she knew coming here had been the right choice.

Slipping past him, Cordelia gravitated toward the fireplace where a warm blaze snapped and danced.

"Where's Isaiah?" Will asked.

"My friend's babysitting. Plus, I told Isaiah what happened, and he's mad at you right now."

"I don't blame him." Will stood beside her at the hearth and gave her braid a light tug. "My delivery a few days ago might have been without finesse, but I meant what I said. Your business is fully thriving and—"

"We're not going to talk about that tonight." She couldn't handle the heavy thoughts another minute. "Let's go do this dinner before I chicken out and change my mind."

"Are you sure you're ready for this? My whole family's there. If you think I'm intrusive, they're professional stream rollers. They're loud and obnoxious and like to play stupid games and eat lots of junk and they'll ask you a million questions. This time I probably won't be able to deflect."

The dimmed lights and the warm fire were doing things to Cordelia's head, wrapping the two of them in a cozy pod that blocked out reality and the rest of the world. She could stay here forever with Will and just exist on ambiance and fantasy. She wondered what he'd do if she took one more step toward him and kissed that faint scar next to his cheek. "I think I can handle your family. I've been rehearsing."

Will traced the ribbon in her hair. "With whom?"

"Isaiah." Cordelia wanted to lean into Will's touch and see where it led. "He's even worse at this conversation stuff than I am."

"What changed your mind?"

"I saw Mr. Mason at the grocery store. It reminded me why I'd committed to this insanity in the first place, and I'm going to see it through." The wood settled in the fireplace with a clatter, and Cordelia stepped back. Away from the flames and from Will. "I haven't gotten much rest lately and that was just kindling to my temper. When we add you, my mom, and no sleepy time, it pretty much makes me combustible."

"I'm sorry I upset you. I know what it's like to have well-meaning people press in, and I should've backed off."

"Throw in a double scoop from Dixie Dairy later, and I accept. Now let's get back to the business at hand."

"You said you'd been rehearsing."

"I'm Broadway ready. We're talking one show a day *plus* a matinee on Sunday."

"I like this new confidence, Daring. Let's do a quick speed round. What's my favorite color?"

"Blue." Like those eyes hot on hers.

"What are my feelings on fish?"

"They belong in the water and not on your plate."

"Favorite band?"

"Spice Girls." His grin sent a zing straight to her toes. "Fine. The Rolling Stones and occasionally U2."

"And why am I crazy about Cordelia Daring?"

Did he mean the good kind of crazy or more of a brain delirium that led to straightjackets and heavy sedation? "Because you suffered head trauma in the explosion?" Her heart seized in her chest as Will moved toward her.

"Because she has the purest heart of any person I know." One of Will's fingers linked with hers. "She gives to people with no expectation of anything in return and bestows mercy when someone don't even deserve it."

"Everyone deserves—"

"Thank you for changing your mind." Lifting her hand, he pressed a kiss to her palm. "Are you ready to be a couple?"

Cordelia was.

And that was becoming her biggest dilemma of all.

CHAPTER SIXTEEN

"**M**AYBE WE COULD go in now, Cordelia?" Will squeezed her hand for the third time.

Cordelia stood next to Will at the end of the driveway, studying the wrap-around porch that seemed to stretch out into the woods. The Sinclair's holiday rental was a rustic, two-story cabin that sat confidently on an expansive acreage, smoke piping from its three chimneys. Surrounded by rolling hills, pine trees, and no visible neighbors, it was perfect for a winter getaway. An image of her and Will snowed-in flashed before Cordelia, and she blinked the hallucination away. She had to quit entertaining these fanciful notions.

"I'm having second and third thoughts," she said. Sure, she'd already met his parents, but there'd been little time for questions and the interview she knew was coming. "Maybe we could tell them I'm sick." It wasn't far from the truth.

"You're gonna do great. I won't leave your side." Will slinked an arm around her waist.

"What if they ask me something I don't know?"

He kissed her cheek, and she could hear the grin. "We'll make out and distract them."

Cordelia turned and regarded him, her stomach stickier than a popcorn ball. "I'm serious."

"So am I."

She could hardly function when he looked at her like that. Somewhere along the way, the line between pretend relationship and *something* had blurred. She didn't know where the line was, and she certainly didn't know what all their *something* entailed. She faced the house again, and yep, these people were still ridiculously rich. "This is so not a *little* vacation house."

"Will!" A willowy, twenty-something ran out the front door with a squeal, then leaped off the porch and propelled herself into Will's arms. "My favorite brother!" She placed smacking kisses on both his cheeks. "I've missed you!"

Will laughed and swung her in a blur of a circle. "Fin."

"Did I hear her call you the favorite?" bellowed another voice from the doorway.

She'd watched enough TV to know the handsome man now exiting the house and entering the front yard fray was Will's brother, Alex.

Will released his sister, letting her feet rest on the ground. "Everyone, meet Cordelia." With a smile that was a brilliant facsimile of adoration, Will returned his hand to her hip and gathered her close. "Cordelia, this is my brother Alex and my sweet sister, Finley."

"It's nice to meet you both," Cordelia said. "I've heard so much about you." But not nearly enough. Alex still lived in Charleston, but Finley had just graduated from college. Her major was acting? No, music. Her boyfriend was the actor. The facts scrambled in her head.

"Come on inside, Cordelia," Alex said. "We can't wait to tell you about the real Will."

With tears in her eyes, Finley hugged her brother one more time. "We're finally all together again."

"Hey, hey." He ruffled her hair like she was five, looking over the top of her head to Alex, who only shrugged. "None of that. Let's go in before you turn into a popsicle."

Inside, Cordelia was instantly squished into hugs from Will's parents before being introduced to Alex's wife, Lucy, who was clearly celebrating the season for two. Will's three-year old nephew and namesake gave Cordelia a fist bump then ran back into the kitchen for more cookies.

"Don't let all this intimidate you," Lucy said, pulling Cordelia to the side as the group had a loud, rambunctious mini-reunion. "The Sinclairs are a wonderful family. They're really close. Well, they were until the bombing. Life fell apart for everyone after that." She sipped from her steaming mug and watched them. "When they found Will, it was a miracle. Like the sun had returned to our lives."

"I can't imagine the shock and relief," Cordelia said.

"I think we all thought things would fall back into place and return to normal."

"But Will isn't letting that happen."

Lucy smiled and tucked a coil of blonde hair behind her ear. "They're a family who's used to being all in each other's business and wound up tightly in each other's lives. But Will still needs time to heal and grieve, you know? I think the Sinclairs struggle with the distance. They've barely seen him since his rescue."

Cordelia watched him across the room as he listened to his sister's animated story. His focus drifted and settled on Cordelia, their eyes locking. She felt like she was in a snow globe, shaken and swirled until she dizzily fell like paper snow. Will gave her a slow wink before returning his attention to Finley at her loud prompt.

"He seems quite smitten with you."

Cordelia found Lucy watching her with a satisfied smile. "Oh, um, we're just dating, and it's still new, and we probably—"

"Is he truly doing okay?" Lucy asked, her brows now knit in concern. "We can't help but be worried."

Cordelia was still mentally churning out definitions of her relationship with Will when she realized the topic had shifted back to Will. "I think Sugar Creek has been good for him."

"So the book's coming along?"

"There's definitely been progress," Cordelia hedged. "It has to be hard to relive the last few years." She couldn't fathom the pain.

"He won't talk about it with us," Lucy said. "Does he mention the bombing to you?"

"A little."

Lucy held her mug close to her chest and watched her family. "I'm glad to know he trusts you with that. He's refused to discuss it with us. Just locked it all inside and withdrew. For months he wouldn't take our calls, wouldn't allow us to visit. He feels incredible guilt over the bombing, but there's no way he could've known they'd be targeted."

"He was a hero," Cordelia said. "He pulled three kids to safety before he was captured. But to Will, it wasn't enough. He feels his celebrity status made the school a target."

Lucy had gone wide eyed and still. "He pulled children to safety?"

Was she not supposed to have mentioned that? "Yes. He saved their lives, not that he finds any redemption in that."

"Will's never said a word, and that wasn't in any of the press. It's like we got the Cliffs Notes version. Cordelia, do you know what I think?"

She wasn't sure she wanted to hear this. "What?"

"I think you have Will's heart."

"No, I—"

"You and your little boy have bewitched him and reached him in a way his family couldn't." Lucy set down her coffee and clasped both Cordelia's shoulders. "Don't give up on him. These Sinclair men are hard to love, but I promise you, it's worth it."

Cordelia watched her walk away, leaving her alone with Lucy's words.

And wishing they were true.

CHAPTER SEVENTEEN

C ORDELIA NEEDED A break.
The Sinclairs were like the mighty sun. She was drawn to their radiance and light, but she feared if she stared at them for too long, she could suffer permanent injury. And, in this case, it was the thorn of envy wedging into Cordelia's heart. This family loved big and loved loud.

From Alex Sinclair's smile-inducing trash talk with Will, to the way Mrs. Sinclair's eyes frequently sought out her Lazarus of a son, lingering as she studied him, a cautious smile on her lips. Cordelia instantly clicked with Lucy, who stood her ground when everyone threw out baby names for a half hour. The woman, who Cordelia learned ran homes for girls who'd aged out of foster care, wanted no part in naming her baby after the Sinclair ancestor Brutus Wilberfink. And then there was Finley and her boyfriend, a dynamic duo if there ever was one. Finley had already composed two songs for blockbuster movies, while her handsome Irishman Beckett Rush had once been a leading actor in successful vampire flicks and now worked behind the camera.

That left Cordelia.

Small-town girl, daughter of the local grouch, and someone who would be voted *Gal With Most Mundane Life* if they'd polled the room.

In three more days Cordelia would deliver her last performance as Will's girlfriend, sticking by his side at his family Christmas Eve dinner. As she had no plans for the night, it was just as well to be with people she genuinely liked, but it would also be bittersweet. But when it was done, she'd give her final bow, allow Will to take her and Isaiah home, then wake up the next morning as Cordelia, the woman *not* dating Will Sinclair.

Slipping out the dining room and onto the back deck, Cordelia clutched her water bottle as if it was something stronger. She poked her hand into the pocket of her sweater where she'd stashed two cookies in case her anxiety prompted a Code Carb.

Above her, the stars twinkled and shimmered, as if unaware of any drama below. Cordelia found the North Star and thought about the very first Christmas, always in awe that she could look on the same guiding light as those seeking the baby Jesus. A little direction would be nice about now. What had started out as a lark, a quick way to earn some Christmas money, had turned into a living thing she couldn't control. From the beginning, Cordelia had assumed she and Will would see very little of one another, but instead they'd been together nearly every day since the agreement. The Will Sinclair she'd watched on TV had been charismatic, articulate, and intelligent, but Cordelia hadn't anticipated the way his smile nearly flat-lined her pulse. Or how he made her laugh just when she needed it most. And good heavens, the sight of that man holding her foster baby in his arms would make the hardest of hearts crumble into tacky, blabbering, *tattoo-his-name-on-questionable-body-parts* love.

And hers was far from the hardest heart.

Cordelia was in big trouble.

The only solution was to guard her feelings and keep her eye on the end date, when she and Will both walked away from the agreement, and life carried on as before.

Yet she knew she'd never be the same.

She had Will Sinclair to blame for that.

No, Cordelia corrected, it was her own stupid fault. Falling for him was completely her doing.

"Hey."

As if manifested by her neurotic meanderings, Will appeared behind her, closing the door with a click to join her on the deck.

"You looked cold." He placed a mug of cocoa on the wooden railing, then draped her forgotten coat around her, his hands lingering on her shoulders. "Are we boring you in there? I promise my dad can talk about more than his new Golden Retriever and how to smoke pork butts."

"Your family is lovely, and you know it." Cordelia leaned against him for only a moment. "And I think you've missed them."

Will propped his elbows on the rail as Finley's boyfriend, Beckett, added more logs to the bonfire below. "I've missed the moments like tonight, when things feel like they used to. But mostly what I get from them outside of the bubble of the holidays is incessant phone calls, smothering texts, and this relentless push for me to be who I was. Tonight nobody's looking at me like I'm fragile or seconds away from disappearing again."

"They love you, Will."

"I know that. I just don't know what to do with this new

version of it."

"Maybe if they saw you more it wouldn't be weird. And they'd be assured you really are okay." She leaned into his side. "Not that you have to be okay. You've been through a horrendous tragedy and—"

"Don't." He turned to face her, his hair blowing in the breeze. "I don't need all that from you too."

Will was right. It wasn't like they were a real couple and Cordelia had to be invested in his well-being. But hadn't they become friends?

Below them Finley walked down the small incline leading to the growing bonfire and hugged her boyfriend. He kissed her soundly, and Cordelia couldn't believe she was less than a hundred feet away from one of Hollywood's favorites.

She whispered her wonder to Will. "Do you know who that is?"

"A guy who can't stop making cow eyes at my sister?"

"Beckett Rush." Would it be rude to take a photo? "*That* is Beckett Rush."

"Yeah, some former child actor, I guess. They've been together since my sister was a senior in high school. My mom said he's now the youngest Oscar-nominated director in movie history."

She watched as the rest of the family trickled out to the Adirondack chairs circling the fire. "Your family's basically the Kennedys of the South. Does every member have a Golden Globe, Super Bowl ring, or Nobel Peace Prize?"

"Don't forget the break-dance trophy I won in second grade." Will frowned when he caught her worrying her bottom lip. "Cordelia, my family's as low-key as it gets. There's absolutely nothing intimidating about those people down there."

"Because you know them."

"And I think I know you." He readjusted the coat sliding from her shoulders, and she tried not to lean in, but the magnet pull was strong. "And you're more of a complement to this family than I am. Big heart, always doing for others, a ridiculous amount of selfless deeds."

"I'm an accountant in small-town Arkansas."

"And a darn good one from what people say. But what you're really good at is bringing people joy with your displays and designs. That Beckett guy's last movie involved a death row inmate, a nuclear winter, and a poetry-writing priest. Not one laser light show." Will anchored his hands on her hips and pressed his forehead to hers. "Now let's go mingle one last time before we go. You do like S'mores, don't you?"

"Yes, but I'm not quite through with my neurotic meltdown." These things couldn't be rushed. "What am I supposed to talk about, Will?"

"How incredible I am." His hold tightened as the laughter from below echoed around them. "Don't forget to use the words gallant, charismatic, and sexiest thing you've ever laid eyes on."

His mother would *so* appreciate that. "I know nothing about football." She set her mug back on the rail. "Or foreign policy or classical music. Or—"

"Cordelia, relax."

She stared into his mercurial eyes, the gray flecks like her kryptonite. "I'm sorry. I'm sleep-deprived, I think I still have spit-up on my shoulder, Isaiah woke up a million times last night, I'm a fish out of water here, and—"

Will's lips on hers ceased all talking.

He stepped closer till even the rising smoke couldn't pass through them, his hands easing up her neck to cup Cordelia's face as if she were an heirloom ornament, breakable and rare. Cordelia sighed as his bottom lip tugged hers, and heat bloomed that had nothing to do with the fire. Her hands made a slow walk up his chest, and her fingers rested on his heart, feeling the steady cadence beneath her palm. Eyes closed, Cordelia reveled in the sensation of being in Will's embrace, his kiss a slow exploration, as if he had all the time in the world. She felt safe, cherished.

But it was a mirage.

Cordelia stepped back, her pulse beating loud, erratic warnings.

"Feeling calmer?" Will asked.

"No."

He swept his lips over hers again. "Now?"

"No."

"Hm." Will shrugged an arrogant shoulder. "Worked for me."

THE CRESCENT MOON levitated over the backyard where the Sinclairs had built a bonfire large enough to send smoke signals to Canada.

"You're not melting your marshmallow." Will pushed Cordelia's stick closer to the fire.

"Stop bossing the poor girl around," Donna Sinclair said. "She can make her S'more any darn way she wants." But she grimaced as Cordelia's marshmallow fell to the ground. "Will, help her, for crying out loud. Don't just stand there."

"Yes, ma'am." He came toward Cordelia with a bag of Stay-Puffs and a gleam in his eye.

"You go back to your spot," Cordelia said, still feeling slightly poleaxed from their earlier kiss. "I'll get the hang of it."

"We'd like you to do it before the New Year." Will dug into the bag. "Allow me to assist." Before she could say Mistletoe Mistake, he scooted in and wrapped his arms around her, guiding Cordelia's hands toward the fire. "You can't be afraid to get close to the flame." His head turned and his cheek brushed hers. "That's where everything gets good."

His words hovered in the air around them.

"Maybe I want to do it my way," Cordelia said.

"Your way isn't working. This just needs a little teamwork."

They stood like that for two more rounds of S'mores, his hands on hers, holding the marshmallow over the fire until it melted into gooey decadence.

"Is that as burned as you like?" Will's lip curled at the black edges Cordelia had requested.

"You say burned, I say perfection." She mashed the white blob into a graham cracker with a candy bar in the middle. "Taste this gourmet, charred creation." She held it towards his mouth, laughing as the chocolate on her fingers smudged Will's cheek.

"Oh, you think that's funny?" He grabbed her wrist and stole the S'more. "You want some chocolate?"

Laughing, Cordelia evaded the melted treat, but not before some of it found its way to her chin. Not ready to lose this fight, she brushed her face against his, laughing when he only drew her closer, threatening retribution.

When Cordelia's lips accidentally brushed against Will's jaw, he stilled. But made no attempt to retreat.

"Will . . ." She saw the heated intent in his eyes, but surely he wouldn't—

"Don't start something you know I'm all too willing to finish." Will captured Cordelia's lips beneath his and kissed her until she gripped his coat and hung on. Her world turned upside down and spiraled at mach speed. Electricity lit her every nerve ending as he pulled her taut against him, afraid if she let go, she'd collapse into a puddle on the ground.

She heard his chest rumble with laughter as he lifted his head and stroked his thumb across her mouth. "You had a little something right there. But I think I got it."

Cordelia was horribly certain if she turned around, she'd find every single Sinclair watching. "You just kissed me."

He looked quite pleased with himself. "I did."

"Right in front of your family."

"Huh." He flicked the zipper of her coat. "Are they still here?"

"Was that a Level One amount of physical contact?"

"No." The corners of his lips tugged upward. "Pretty sure we just graduated to Level Two."

Heaven help her if they even dipped a toe in Three. "I think being with your family has overwhelmed you and—"

"I think I've wanted to do that since I first saw you trespassing on my lawn."

"Oh." Her heart melted like the marshmallow held over a flame.

His sister-in-law's words came back to Cordelia. "*I think you have Will's heart.*"

Bur surely that wasn't true.

Though there was no point in denying it any longer.

Will Sinclair certainly held hers.

CHAPTER EIGHTEEN

C ORDELIA READ WILL'S text for the tenth time that day.

I'm picking you up at six.

Let's crunch numbers all night long.

Will had been serious about attending her company Christmas party. Why would he want to go with her? *She* didn't even want to go. Had he ever heard her boss sing "Love Shack" karaoke? It was not the bow you wanted to stick on the end of your year.

Last evening's dinner with his family had been like freefalling from an airplane. She'd been exhilarated by the sweetness of it all—the food, the conversation, the laughter. It had done her heart good to see the Sinclair family circle around Will and enjoy each other, not to mention the way they'd included her. But then Will had kissed her, and she no longer understood the rules. Gravity, space, and time no longer held her upright, and she woke up this morning still flailing in the air.

Were they a couple now? Or was she just his Sugar Creek fling—Will's crutch as he hobbled away from his family and deadlines? Cordelia had never been someone's fling, so she wasn't sure what the signs were or if she was emotionally stable enough to handle it. When she loved, she loved with her whole heart, and couldn't walk way as if it had all meant nothing.

Not that she loved him.

That was ridiculous. Nobody fell in love over eleven days.

Did they?

Her doorbell rang twice, and Cordelia scooped up Isaiah, then opened the door.

Will didn't say hello. He simply scowled. "Your dress is black."

"Yes." She patted Isaiah's back as cold air rushed in.

"You're wearing black to a Christmas party." Stepping inside, Will felt Cordelia's forehead, then ran his hands down her back.

She squirmed under his touch. "What are you doing?"

"Looking to see that it at least has a battery pack."

"My dress doesn't light up."

"No tinsel in your hair, plain pearl earrings, and not one blinking, music-abusing device on you? Cordelia, I think this might be early signs of the flu."

Cordelia wasn't sick, but she sure wasn't herself. For the first time, Isaiah had slept through the night, a feat that should've made the angels sing. Instead Cordelia had lain awake, counting sheep and romantic complications, catching about an hour of rest and a significant stockpile of anxieties. Weren't they going to talk about the kiss? Talk about the fact that he'd smooched her right in front of his family? The numbers girl in her wanted to know what the value of that moment was to him. What category did she file it under, or did she just declare it a miscellaneous expense?

"Are you sure you want to suffer through the party?" Cordelia asked, allowing herself a moment to appreciate the sight of Will in a dark suit and cranberry tie. He looked like a GQ model and would surely be the best looking man at the party. And to think, he'd be with her.

"I'm certain," Will said. "It's charades and Pictionary night at my parents' and I'd much rather hang out with you than try to decipher my dad's inappropriate use of stick figures." He pulled her to him and first kissed her cheek, then Isaiah's. "Is the baby going?"

"Yes. My sitter canceled." Her raised eyebrows dared him to reconsider his attendance.

"Works for me." Will took the diaper bag and the wriggling baby from her arms. "Hey, there, little man. Are you ready for your first office party?"

Isaiah wore a red plaid shirt, denim bow tie, and itty bitty khakis. Buying baby clothes had become Cordelia's new hobby, and unfortunately for her budget, she was way too good at it.

"Are there any jealous ex-boyfriends at this shindig I need to know about?" Will asked as they walked to his car.

"No." Cordelia put the baby into his seat. "Though Sean Bartowski once asked me to have dinner with him."

"That never went anywhere?"

She buckled herself in and clutched the diaper bag in her lap. "Turns out Sean lives with his mother, and the two go every-where together. And that includes dates at the gas station all-you-can-eat buffet."

"So the bar's set pretty low." Will turned the key, and the car roared to life. "Best odds I've had in a long time."

"Is Isaiah getting too heavy?" Cordelia asked. "Your arms are probably tired. Let me take him."

Frank Sinatra sang "Joy to the World" while Will drank his second glass of cranberry punch and held a sleeping Isaiah. The punch wasn't spiked, and not for the first time, he wished it had been. "I've got this." He waved a hand toward the dance floor of the hotel conference room where a group of people stepped and snapped. "Go mingle with your people. Your number nerds. Your calculator community."

Cordelia bit into a glittery sugar cookie as she regarded him. "Not without you." She licked her glossed lips. "We're one of those inseparable couples."

"Are we?"

"Yes. Completely annoying. We're probably a few days away from creating a joint Facebook profile and dressing alike on the weekends."

Will cradled a sleeping Isaiah in his arms. "I'm gonna look great in a ponytail."

Cordelia had been an antsy mess all evening, and he was finally rewarded with a smile. Will wondered if she knew how that smile made people feel. She lit up a room just by walking into it and put everyone at ease. Even when wearing a coal black dress. What was up with that? It would've looked glamorous on anyone else, but on Cordelia, bright, sparkly Cordelia, it looked like something she'd wear to a funeral. She wasn't acting like herself, and he wasn't sure why. Maybe after a year off, being back with her coworkers felt strange. It certainly didn't feel strange to the staff of Fillmore and Associates. Upon Cordelia's arrival, she'd been swarmed like Beyoncé and hugged till he thought she might deflate. Her coworkers clearly loved her. But who wouldn't?

Even in that strangely drab dress, Cordelia looked amazing. Will had met a lot of chic A-list celebrities, interviewed exotic female dignitaries, and visited nearly every country on the planet. But no woman in the world had affected him like the sight of Cordelia tonight. Will wanted to ditch the accountants, put Cordelia and Isaiah on a plane, and fly them to his favorite restaurant in Charleston, tucking them away in a dim corner table where it would be just the three of them. No Christmas trappings. No nosy onlookers. He'd hold her hand during dinner, watch the candle reflection dance in her eyes, and ply her with some of his favorite travel stories until her heard her laugh and saw the dimples in her smile.

The techno music wound down, and the Mr. Fillmore grabbed a microphone from a stand. Her boss wrestled with the cord then smiled at the shushing crowd. "Is this thing on?" The mic squealed in protest.

With sleepy eyes, Isaiah lifted his head from Will's shoulder and began to wail. Before Will could deliver even one gentle pat, Cordelia took the baby and held him to her, frantically rocking him like she was about to send him airborne.

"Shhh, Isaiah." She rubbed his little back. "It's okay. Shhh."

"I'd like to congratulate everyone on a successful year," Mr. Fillmore said. "We've had our most profitable year yet, and I owe it all to you, my fabulous employees." He paused for a polite round of applause, which startled Isaiah even more. "Not only do we have Christmas bonuses to celebrate this year, but we have some long awaited promotions." Chatter erupted all around them. Apparently this was a hot topic. "I'd like to announce a full-time position for our university intern. Misti Cotton, get on up here and take a bow."

Isaiah's lungs went into overdrive, and Cordelia wore a look of mild panic. "I'm going to take him into the hall," she said, gathering up her diaper bag and quickly walking away.

"Is that Cordelia Daring I see?" Mr. Fillmore squinted behind his rimless glasses as his tie flashed red and green. "Don't rush off yet, Cordelia."

She swiveled and faced them, wearing a wobbly smile on her lips and a screaming Isaiah on her shoulder.

"Ladies and gentlemen, Fillmore and Associates couldn't get along without this woman right here. I should know because we've tried." He paused to give Isaiah's volume a chance to diminish. "Can I present to you the next audit manager and vice-president of our company, Cordelia Daring!"

Will walked toward her, prepared to relieve her of Isaiah. But before he could get there, Cordelia's wide eyes found his. She gave the slightest shake of her head, then bolted. Ran off like she was hoping to qualify for the Olympics.

A few minutes later Will found Cordelia on a couch in the hotel lobby. She had Isaiah tucked into the crook of one arm while she held a bottle to his lips. Sitting with her legs crossed, she bobbed one foot with a spastic, angry rhythm.

"Hey." Will approached slowly, as if coming upon a wounded fawn. "What happened in there?"

"Isaiah's not feeling well," she said. "I need to get him

home."

Will looked at the wide-awake baby, happily chugging milk. "Does he have fever?"

"No."

"Did he throw up?"

"No." Cordelia sniffed. "But I can tell he doesn't feel good. And that room is crawling with people. Germy ones who might want to touch Isaiah or sneeze in his direction. And who knows if we're all on the same page about sufficient hand-washing. Will, did you know that some people don't suds up above the wrist?"

Will had been raised with a sister. He knew when to keep his mouth shut and not bring up something ridiculous like logic and reality. "If you want to stay at the party, I can take care of Isaiah. It sounds like you were about to have a moment in there."

"No." She stood, still feeding the baby. "Let's just go home." Plaintive eyes met Will's. "Please."

Cordelia had little to say on the ride home and shot down any of Will's attempts to talk about the party. The watered down punch was apparently a safe topic, but when he broached her promotion, she cranked up the radio and punished him with the rap version of "Frosty the Snowman."

Sleet began to pelt the windshield just as he steered the car into her driveway. Will shimmied out of his coat and held it over Cordelia as she gathered the baby and walked inside.

"I'm going to get Isaiah in his pajamas and put him down." Cordelia kicked out of her heels, made a fast bottle, then padded down the hallway.

Fifteen minutes later, Will had rummaged through her

kitchen until he found chamomile tea. He grabbed the mug and walked down the hall till he spied Isaiah's bedroom. The room glowed with a star night light, casting enchanting shadows on the walls. Cordelia sat in an oversized glider, fast asleep. In her arms she cradled her foster son, who nestled toward her, his little hands folded as if in prayer.

Will took a drink of Cordelia's tea and just watched her, the strange sensation of happiness drifting upward to the vicinity of his heart. Her cheek pressed against the chair, Cordelia looked slightly disheveled, completely exhausted, and yet blissfully content to hold this small baby. It was a tableau begging to be painted, a photo waiting to be taken. A scene lit by a tiny plug-in light and God himself.

He set the mug down then gently eased Isaiah from Cordelia's grip, marveling at the way the child radiated warmth and some fathomless, intangible thing that wrapped around them both and soothed Will's unsettled soul. Isaiah curled his fingers beneath his chin as Will placed him back into the crib.

The children who'd perished in the bombing had once looked like this—small, innocent, oblivious to the evils of the world. If only he could turn back time and fix it all. Never have opened another school, never have gone to Durnama. How many parents had come home to empty bedrooms with nothing but memories of nights like this?

"Will?"

He turned to find Cordelia watching him. "Go back to sleep."

She smiled and stretched. "I can't tell you how many times I've nodded off in here." Her voice was a hushed whisper in the room. "I could watch Isaiah by the hour. He's perfect, isn't he?"

Will let his finger graze the velvety softness of Isaiah's cheek. "He's. . ." He struggled to find the right adjective, but none would do the child justice. "He is perfect." Dragging himself away from the crib, Will loosened his tie, then sat down on the carpet beside Cordelia's chair. "Are we going to talk about tonight?"

Her rocking stilled. "What about it?"

"Your promotion. You jetting off like the building was on fire."

"I'll explain to my boss on Monday. I'm sure he'll understand."

Was this how Cordelia felt when she tried to talk to him? "Help me understand."

She rubbed the back of her neck, the fatigue back in her eyes. "You're saying my exit was a little out of proportion to the moment?"

"Maybe I was the only one who noticed."

She picked up a fuzzy stuffed bear, held it to her face, and groaned. "What is wrong with me?"

"Besides sleep-deprivation and a questionable collection of Christmas sweaters?"

"One of those qualities would make me a slam dunk on Match.com."

He didn't even want to think of her on any dating site. "Let's lay out the facts here." He leaned toward her, his voice church-sermon low. "You got a big promotion, and instead of going up to accept it, you ran out of the room."

"I think we've already covered that."

"Do you need any more confirmation you don't want to return to the accounting gig?"

"This again?"

"The evidence is really starting to stack up."

Cordelia massaged a spot above her temple before meeting his gaze. They were two people having a whispered conversation in a darkened nursery. It was intimate and strange. Yet somehow felt just right.

"The promotion came as a shock is all," she finally said. "It would be like ABC announcing on *Good Morning America* that you'd been hired to host—without your knowledge you were even in the running."

"You didn't know a promotion to vice-president was an option?"

She ran a finger over the teddy bear's pink nose. "It had been dangled a few times, but I thought Mr. Fillmore was just saying things to woo me back. I figured I was too young for him to truly consider it. The last person he made VP was fifty-five and had already had two knee replacements. How could I compete with that?"

"Are you taking the job?"

She turned her head, her eyes lingering on Isaiah. "I don't know."

"How long do you have to decide?"

"One week."

"I think you should turn him down."

"You're not making my house payment."

Fair enough. "Don't sell yourself short, Cordelia."

"I don't think the title of vice-president is anything too

shabby."

"No, it's a huge accomplishment." Will stood and extended a hand to help Cordelia to her feet. "But the best job can be the worst—if it's not what you're put here to do."

"Remind me." She patted his chest. "How's that book of yours coming along?"

He tamped down the anger that wanted to push like a geyser to the surface. "It's fine"

"Is it?" She angled her head, her hair swaying with sass. "What chapter did you say you're on?"

He felt like he'd been caught cheating by his teacher. "I don't know. Maybe chapter eight."

"Weren't you on chapter seven last week?"

"Writing a book isn't as easy as you might think."

"Neither is walking away from a solid paycheck." Her smile was a swift dart of comeuppance. "I'm so grateful my fake boyfriend understands."

CHAPTER NINETEEN

O N DECEMBER TWENTY-FOURTH, snowflakes fluttered in the air like kisses from the clouds.

To Cordelia, it was the perfect accent to Christmas, and if she'd staged the day, she would've ordered the snow herself. While Isaiah bounced and played in his Jumparoo beside her, Cordelia peeled the backing from her laser-cut letters and carefully stuck them in the display window of Frannie's Cupcakes, her friend's store set to open next month.

"What are you still doing here?" Frannie Nelson paused as she carried a stack of boxes to a shelf. "We agreed you'd work a couple of hours then get on home. Besides the bad weather coming, it's Christmas Eve. Don't you have a date with that handsome Will Sinclair?"

"I do." Cordelia held a level over the letters, double checking their alignment. "But that's later." Why rush the day? The sooner she went to the Sinclair Christmas Eve dinner, the sooner it was all over.

Cordelia had tried not to think about it all week, but time had a funny way of moving on whether you wanted to or not. By the end of this evening, her deal with Will would expire, and their fake romance would be the stuff of diary pages and faded recollections. She told herself it was for the best, but nothing that beneficial should hurt this badly.

"The shop's going to look dy-no-mite," Frannie said. "When people walk by the windows, they'll have to stop in." She'd sold her cupcakes from a food trailer and turned into an overnight sensation. Now she was ready to go pro.

Cordelia watched Isaiah spit out his pacifier as he smacked a rattle with his hand. "I can't wait to get started."

"Well, waiting's exactly what you're gonna do." Frannie's head zig-zagged with attitude. "I don't want to see you back in here until well after the holiday."

Cordelia's design involved a display of papier-mâché cupcakes in colors of turquoise, black, and white. The confections would stack to form the Eiffel Tower with cupcake flowers blooming along the border and gossamer sprinkles raining over the scene. She'd recruited some students from the local university's art department, and their sample work had been exquisite.

"One of my customers said you got a big promotion last weekend at Fillmore and Associates," Frannie said.

The town probably knew Cordelia's bra size and what she'd had for breakfast. Sugar Creek allowed no secrets, and some days it grated to no end. "Yes, it's an exciting prospect."

Frannie chuckled and ran her fingers over her updo wig. "You said that as if referring to a walk before the firing squad. Girl, I know it's scary to go out on your own and take the road less traveled. But you're good at what you do, and you shouldn't waste that gift on a desk job."

Cordelia picked a burp cloth from the floor and slid it into her diaper bag. "But your cupcake business is your second career. If you go under, it's not like you're going to lose your retirement or social security. It's not quite the same."

"I'm not talking about cupcakes," Frannie said. "When I joined the CIA there were few women in the bureau. Sylvie and I were on a secret elite team, and we didn't know from one day to the next if we'd survive. You know what my friends were doing? Getting married and having babies, that's what. And sometimes I thought I should quit because of what was expected of me. But I understood I had a gift and a calling. God gave me eyes in the back of my head, a brain that works overtime, and a nose for intrigue. So I stuck it out and stayed in the CIA. It wasn't easy and I sacrificed a lot, but there's nothing like operating in the flow of the divine—that high of doing what you love. Do you hear what I'm saying?"

She did. "I'm so afraid to fail, Frannie." Cordelia thought of her mother. "I don't want to hear 'I told you so.'"

Frannie picked up the baby and kissed his chubby cheek. "Failure is what keeps us alive. It's what tells the world we're still trying. Cordelia, it looks to me like the good Lord has passed you the basketball for one glorious assist. You're under the rim with a clear shot. Now, I suggest you take it. Regret is a bitter pill that never goes down." She wiped the drool from her shirt. "Looks like you got company."

Cordelia turned around to see Ananya waving from the sidewalk outside.

"I'll just take this sweet baby in the kitchen and introduce him to some pots and pans," Frannie said.

The bell on the door jingled as Ananya stepped inside.

One look at her face, and Cordelia's stomach folded. "What's wrong?"

Ananya unwrapped the scarf from her neck, her mouth set in a grim line. "Isaiah's mom dropped out of the prison rehab program yesterday."

"So she'll either change her mind tomorrow or get another chance." Cordelia had learned there were lots of do-overs when it came to bio parents on a plan to regain custody of their children.

"If she doesn't do rehab, the minimum sentence for her drug charges is ten years," Ananya said. "She's made up her mind, and this isn't something a local judge can fix."

"So the kids are in foster care indefinitely?"

Ananya took a loud breath then shook her head. "Isaiah's mother has terminated her rights."

Cordelia heard a baby's squeal from the back, and it echoed in her ears. "What do you mean?"

"I mean Sabra Mason has surrendered her children to the state."

She needed to sit down. Cordelia reached a hand for the wall and eased to the floor, her legs forming a pretzel, just like her thoughts. "What's going to happen?"

"Steve Mason will become a father of four."

"And Isaiah?"

Her friend squatted beside her. "I know you're a foster-only home, but I want you to give this some thought. Take a few days. A week. I can't give you much more than that, but I want you to consider adopting Isaiah."

"I'm not ready," Cordelia said. "I'm not married. I don't make six figures. I can't even remember to floss on a daily basis. Isaiah needs more than that."

"Here we are!" Frannie reappeared, holding a grinning Isaiah. "He fell in love with my rubber spatula, so Auntie Frannie gave him two."

Cordelia took the outstretched baby into her arms, and he tucked his head beneath her chin.

"You're wrong, Cordelia." Ananya looked at the two and gave a watery smile. "From what I see, Isaiah has everything he needs."

CHAPTER TWENTY

C ORDELIA SAT IN her car in the Sullivan's driveway and contemplated not going inside.

If she didn't go in, then could Christmas Eve actually happen? What if she didn't want the bargain with Will to be over? She didn't need the rest of the money. Sure, her car had died twice on the way there, but maybe she just needed to buy a bicycle and give up her dream of reliable transportation. The money Will had already given her had purchased a king's ransom in presents and necessities for Steve Mason and the kids. Wasn't that enough?

Will could keep the other half of her payment, and she'd leave here and go on her not-so-merry way.

Knock. Knock.

She startled at the face peering in her window.

"Cordelia?" Chunky snowflakes dove and danced around Will's shoulders. "Are you going to come in now or would you like more time for one of your neurotic meltdowns?"

If Will ended things with her tonight, her heart would leave a trail of shattered pieces all the way home. She'd just gotten news that her foster baby needed a forever mother. *And* she had two jobs, but like some tragically boring twist on *The Bachelor*, could only choose one. But yeah, this was just another neurotic meltdown. *Don't mind me!*

Will opened the car door and blocked the wind from whooshing inside. "Hey." He brushed his thumb across her cheek, where she knew there were remnants of mascara she'd cried off at some point on the way over. "Those people inside that house adore you. There's nothing to get stressed about."

Did Will adore her? "I've had a really bad day."

He glanced down and took in her red sweater. "Does that Christmas tree light up?"

Normally this outfit was her holiday piece de resistance. "The star on top flashes in ten different colors and the tinsel glows in the dark."

"I like how the tree skirt is a real. . .skirt."

She knew it was awful. That's what made it so wonderful. "What are we doing, Will?"

"Contemplating how many batteries you go through a week."

Cordelia was just going to come out and say it. "I mean us."

He reached for her hand and helped her out of the car. "First, we're going to have dinner. Then we're headed to the church for a candlelight service. Then we're gonna talk."

"Let's talk now." Because if he was breaking up with her, she wanted to leave her pie in the car so she'd have something to binge eat later.

Will kissed her, a feather-light touch of his lips. "I'm gonna need more time than we've got."

"Will, I—"

Isaiah chose that moment to hit a perfect high C, screaming the song of a hungry boy.

"How about we take Isaiah inside and get you both fed." Will reached for her hand and pressed his lips to her cheek. "But later—we will have that talk."

ONE HOUR INTO the evening, and Cordelia was coming apart like a rose bush in a hurricane.

The family gathered at a large harvest table in a dining room big enough to swallow her entire home. They passed the desserts around, laughing over memories of holidays gone by. Donna Sinclair held Isaiah and didn't even flinch when he grabbed her hair. She just kissed his curly head, gave him a bite of his pureed squash, and sang softly near his ear. Like the grandmother that he deserved.

To add to her emotional claustrophobia, Will had sat so close to Cordelia in dinner, she elbowed him in the ribs every time she took a bite. He'd draped his arm over the back of her chair, and twice during the meal he leaned over and kissed her. Either the green bean casserole really revved him up or he truly did hold her in some affection.

But it was all too much. Cordelia had barely been able to choke down the turkey, and the potatoes had tasted like Elmer's glue on her tongue.

"Excuse me. I'm going to get a refill." She tossed her napkin to the table, grabbed her water glass, and escaped to the kitchen. Needing to keep her hands busy lest they perform "I love you" in sign language, Cordelia ran some water in the sink and squeezed a figure-eight of dish soap into the depths.

"I'm stuffed. I won't want to eat for a week." Lucy Sinclair walked in with an empty plate in one hand while her pregnant belly protruded beneath her other. "Or at least for another hour. I'm going to need the recipe for your coconut cream pie."

"It was my grandmother's," Cordelia said, scrubbing at a bowl with a rag and wishing she could be alone.

If Lucy thought it strange their guest was doing dishes, she didn't say a word. But she did grab a tea towel, roll up her sleeves, and offer to help. "I can dry." She took the bowl from Cordelia and buffed all the water away. "You know, I've only known Will since his return, but I've never seen him smile as much as he has tonight."

Glad someone was happy. Cordelia could barely function.

"You two look good together," Lucy said. "Did you say you've only known one another a few months?"

"Uh-huh." She scraped at a platter, desperate to prevail over its dried-on grease.

Lucy dried a glass with a sweep of the towel. "Things appear to be moving fast."

"Maybe it's just the romance of the holidays," Cordelia said.

"Is it?" Lucy smiled. "You seem to care for my brother-in-law."

"Of course I do. What's not to love? I mean *like*. Like is what I mean. What's not to like?" She should've eaten some dessert.

"How was it you met again?"

Cordelia reviewed the script tattooed in her head. "A party at Noah and Emma Kincaid's."

"Ah."

What did that mean?

Lucy folded the tea towel in half and leaned her hip against the counter. "Noah's wife Emma happens to be a good friend of mine."

A plate slipped from Cordelia's hands and splashed into the sudsy water.

"She speaks highly of you," Lucy said. "Strangely enough, she didn't recall a dinner party that Will had ever attended. Or you."

"She . . .she must be mistaken. Will and I were at her house. Eating dinner. And in a party-like fashion. There were people there. Lots of them. I tend to fade in crowds, and she probably didn't see me. I have social camouflage." She laughed a little too loudly. "I can usually be found talking to the host's dogs and standing near the house plants." Was it hot in here or just too much lying? "But that's where we met."

Lucy smiled, but her eyes sparked with something more than humor. "Emma can be a little scatterbrained. I'm sure she just forgot."

"Right. It happens. I should probably go back in the dining room. Rejoin the fun."

"My own meet-cute was a little more dramatic," Lucy said as she reached for another dish to dry. "Four years ago I was in serious need of money for my girl's shelter, and this cocky, former NFL player found himself in desperate need of an image makeover for his run for Congress. So we pretended to be engaged and then accidentally . . .fell in love."

Cordelia replayed the confession in head twice. "You did?"

"Yep. Craziest thing I've ever done in my life." She quirked one brow. "But also the most fun I've ever had with another human being."

"And quite the story to tell your children one day," Cordelia said.

"Maybe." Lucy regarded Cordelia with a tilt of her head. "Actually, I've never shared that story outside the family. You'll keep that between us, won't you?"

"Yes. Sure." Cordelia decided as nice as Lucy was, she wouldn't bet against her in a game of poker. "So why did you tell me?"

"I liked you immediately, Cordelia. And I think we might have a lot in common." She walked away, only to hesitate in the doorway. "It's funny, but I believe sometimes the best love stories . . .are the ones we write ourselves."

CHAPTER TWENTY-ONE

THE SNOW HAD gone from quaint Norman Rockwell to an Ozark white out.

While Cordelia and the family sat in the living room playing dominoes and drinking coffee, Will stood at the window in a spare bedroom, held the phone to his ear, and watched the weather rapidly deteriorate. He knew Cordelia would want to get on the road and get Isaiah home. She'd planned on taking her gifts to the Mason children in the morning, but with a band of ice moving through later, he doubted that would happen.

"I know this isn't your normal fare," said the voice on the other end of the phone. "But we think you'd be a good fit."

When Will saw Anderson Blackwell's number on his display only minutes ago, he'd slipped away to take the call. He'd been dealing directly with the executive producer, and he knew the man was ready to finalize a deal.

"It's definitely unlike anything I've done," Will said. "But I think this could be a good first step back to the news. And you're right. A morning show will be a . . ." Smiley, fluff-fest of surface-level chit-chat. "A new challenge." His head throbbed at the producer's next question. "The autobiography? The book won't get in the way. I canceled the project yesterday and returned the advance." He tapped his finger against the windowsill. "I can be in New York in two weeks. Is that enough time? I've got some loose ends to tie up here and—"

Hearing a noise behind him, Will turned.

Cordelia stood in the doorway, her body tense and her eyes a condemnation.

"Cordelia—"

She turned and left, a blur of escape.

He had to talk to her. "Um, yeah, Anderson, sounds good. I'll call you Monday, okay?" Will slipped the phone in his pocket and went in pursuit of Cordelia, cursing himself for assuming it wouldn't matter to her. Once again, he'd handled everything all wrong. "Cordelia?"

He took a detour through the living room, then beelined for the kitchen. "Anyone seen Cordelia?"

His brother inclined his head toward the front door. "Just walked outside."

"You know it's snowing, right?" his mother asked. "She refused our offer to take her home."

He didn't bother to respond, but raced out of the house, running into the driveway as Cordelia slammed her car door shut. "Wait."

She started her geriatric car and put it in reverse.

"I know you heard me." Will was perfectly aware he sounded like a raving lunatic. "Cordelia!" He leapt in front of her just as she threw it in drive, the car screeching to a halt. Her window slid down.

"Are you nuts?" she yelled. "I could've hit you." Snow collected in her hair as it fell sideways from the sky.

"Where are you going?"

She leaned an elbow out the window. "I overhear *that* phone call and you want to discuss my next destination? There's nothing else you'd like to say to me?"

Will held up his hands in surrender and walked to her door. "Get out and talk to me, Cordelia. Please."

"You want to talk? We can talk right here."

"It's freezing outside. And you don't need to be driving in this weather."

"Then let me go before it gets worse."

But he couldn't. She had to hear him out. "I know you're mad."

"I'm not mad. A *real* girlfriend would be mad. So I'm just fine."

She said *fine* like he'd once heard a president say *nuclear*. "I can commute on the weekends. You can fly up to New York."

At that she got out of the car, slamming the door once again. The snow picked up in intensity, as if matching her fury. "When were you going to tell me, Will?"

"I—"

"Yeah, that's what I thought. And what about your book?"

"Who cares about the book?" His volume lifted toward the trees.

"I care. The people who love you and want to know your story care. The kids who need to hear about a hero—"

"Stop. Don't say that." His throat hurt as words collected there. "I can't write it." Will turned his head, horrified to hear his voice break. "I'm not writing that book."

She closed the distance between them. "Why?"

"Because it's too much. I thought I could do it, and I can't.

The chapters I've yet to write would be pages and pages about the kids—before and after the blast. I don't want to go back there. I can't see their faces and keep reliving that day."

Her hand rested on his chilled arm. "Then don't do the project, but let it go for the right reasons. You saved lives by bringing those children a chance at an education. You rescued kids from the flames."

"It was my—"

"It wasn't your fault. Stop saying that. It's a lie you've bought into, and it's wrong. I'm sorry for what happened. I can't begin to imagine the horror of everything you've been through, but you've suffered enough. You were set free nine months ago, but you're still sitting in a prison of your own making. Walk out the door, Will." She pointed toward the house. "Your family's waiting on you. You have this wonderful, amazing family, and you don't even see them."

"And you?"

"What about me?" Tears pooled in her eyes. That was something at least. "We were never real."

"That's not true. I know you feel something for me. Now who's believing a lie?"

She brushed a hand across her nose. "You're out of here in two weeks. I heard you say it. And for what?"

"I got an offer I couldn't refuse."

"For the morning news."

"Yes. UTV. It's one of the premiere news cable networks."

"I know what it is."

"I'll be co-anchoring the *Daylight Update* show."

She stared at him like he had lost his ever-loving mind. "You earned a Pulitzer nomination for your writing, an Edward R. Murrow for your reporting, and probably a countless mantel-full of accolades I've never even heard of, and you think that's going to satisfy you?"

"It's a start. It'll be something different."

"You'll be bored after the first celebrity gossip story you have to read. You're completely wimping out. You keep telling me to take a chance on my design business, and just when I think I might, you play it safe with your smiley talk show."

"It's not a talk show. It's—"

"It's not in the guts of a foreign country or in the underbelly of D.C."

"Maybe I can't be that reporter anymore." Fear punched his every word. "What if I don't want to be constantly wondering when the next bomb's going off?"

"You're detonating your own life."

"Oh, tell me all about that, Cordelia *Daring*."

"Don't make this about me. I've listened for days while you preached against the evils of settling. And now look at you."

"This is a multi-million dollar contract. If I'm settling, it sure comes with a lot of zeroes." He hated the smug drip of his tone, but she had him cornered and stripped bare.

"Yeah, it's a lot of money. You're very lucky." She brushed snow from her lashes. "And while I know what it's like to take a job for the paycheck, that's not why you're doing it. You don't care about money. I've seen your work for years. It's all about the thrill of the story, your pursuit of truth. I can understand not being ready to write about the experience or get back in the war zones, but this job isn't you."

"It is for now."

She shoved her hands in her pockets and shivered against the rising wind. "When were you going to tell me you were leaving?"

He hesitated one second too long.

"I see," she said. "Let me guess, the night before you took off? Or perhaps you'd call before your connecting flight?"

"I care about you, Cordelia."

"This has been an illusion, hasn't it? Just a game you played that I allowed."

"Don't say that."

"I knew it wasn't real, but I let my heart get wrapped up in it anyway. We were nothing more than a mutual agreement."

"We're more than that."

"No, I don't think we are." She sniffed and zipped her coat. "We're two messed up people who helped each other out." She walked to him then, a fierce warrior angel. Standing on her toes, Cordelia kissed his frozen cheek. "I truly hope you find what you're looking for. Merry Christmas, Will."

"Wait." His hand stopped her, as his pulse thrummed with panic. She paused, and he knew she was waiting for the words to turn this all around, to slice open a vein and bleed honesty and gutted fear. "You're mine till Christmas. That was the deal."

He saw her quit, felt her withdraw. "The deal's off."

"You're just going to walk away from this?" From their arrangement, from what they had?

"In two weeks you were going to walk away from us and tie up all your loose ends." The wind howled as she stepped away. "I'm just beating you to it."

CHAPTER TWENTY-TWO

T HE CHURCH SMELLED like drip coffee and carpet shampoo. Instrumental Christmas music played lightly from overhead speakers while shadows danced in the dim lights. The rows of seats were already filled with families packed shoulder to shoulder, wearing everything from their Sunday finest to children in pajamas. His mother spotted him and waved him down like she was trying to get the attention of a 747. He could see her joy and relief from clear across the sanctuary, tightening the slipknot around his gut.

After the argument with Cordelia, she hadn't expected him to show up. Hadn't expected him to mean it when he said he'd follow them to the church.

Shame took a quick stab in the general vicinity of his retired conscience. Will had become the prodigal son, the one they couldn't count on. He knew he'd avoided his family more than usual this year, but it had just been too much. Their looks of pity, as if he might shatter into shards if they said the wrong thing or hugged too tightly. Maybe he hadn't returned from Afghanistan as his old self, but his family wasn't the same either. Only they couldn't see that. And he didn't know how to tell them.

He sidestepped a toddler wearing angel wings and wove his

way through the crush of revelers toward his parents' row. For a snowy night, the place was surprisingly packed.

Will hadn't entered a church since before his capture. Almost five years had passed since he'd celebrated Christmas, held a Bible, or heard the beauty of a hymn. Growing up, his mama had made sure her children were in a pew every Sunday. But as Will had sat in that darkened cell, he'd wondered at the existence of God. Where had God been when a bomb had been thrown? Why had he spared Will and not a child? He'd prayed many days in captivity, but hadn't gotten any answers. His rescue had come, and maybe that had been Divine, but no answers had ever followed. And now he just wondered if God heard his prayer to bring Cordelia back.

"Will!" His sister dropped her boyfriend's hand and exited the row to throw her arms around Will's neck. "I knew you'd join us." She squeezed tighter, as if needing a moment to convince herself he wasn't going to evaporate.

Alex gave him a smile and nod, and his father clasped his shoulder after he sat down.

His dad checked his fancy smart watch. "I don't see what's holy about church at midnight. Pretty sure even Jesus is in bed already."

His mother reached across her husband and patted Will's knee. "I've got some sugar cookies for you in my purse. Freshly baked."

"That woman's bag is straight out of *Mary Poppins*," his dad said. "She's got cookies, a full serving set, and three wrapped gifts—just in case."

No one asked about Cordelia, for which Will thanked the

probably-sleeping-baby Jesus.

A wholesome looking fellow in a red sweater and green bow tie took to the stage. "Welcome to the Sugar Creek Community Church. We're so happy to celebrate Christmas together. Please join us as we sing."

Everyone stood as the worship band struck the first chords of "Silent Night."

Will glanced about, realizing that once again, he was surrounded by children. Shouldn't they be tucked in bed, waiting for Santa Claus?

That familiar tightness, that anxiety that gripped his heart like a vice now barely even squeezed. He looked around again. Even tentatively smiled at the infant watching him from a father's shoulder in the seat before him. He had baby Isaiah to thank for that, he supposed. Man, he would miss that kid.

When the song ended, Cordelia's book club friend Frannie Nelson took the mic. She wore a green dress with a rhinestone Christmas wreath on her chest, and Will knew Cordelia would've loved it. But when Frannie opened her mouth to sing, there was nothing flashy or silly about it. The woman had to be kin to Aretha Franklin. She gave new life to "Joy to the World," and the entire congregation got back to their feet without prompting.

"Let earth receive her King. Let every heart prepare Him room. And heaven and nature sing. And heaven and nature sing . . ."

Will sat spellbound, barely hearing the words, but letting Frannie's voice take him somewhere else. When she sang, he could almost feel unshackled, if only for a moment. His shoulders lifted, as if the heavy burden he'd carried levitated at her words. He wanted joy to be possible for someone like him. He just didn't know how to get there. Cordelia made it look so easy. She came at life with a gusto the old Will once had.

All too soon, the song and singer reached a crescendo, coming to a close. Will thought he might as well go home. The Lord had arrived for a few minutes, and Miss Frannie had ushered Him in.

The pastor returned to the pulpit and promised he'd be brief. Will's father grunted his approval.

"The first Christmas was a night of not just wonder—but also of *wander*." Like a good speaker, Pastor Bowtie let his eyes sweep the room. "Mary and Joseph traveled many miles before Jesus was born. Some believe the Wise Men might've followed the North Star for months. Even the shepherds left their flocks and took off on foot." He nodded to his ushers, who began to pass out white candles. "I don't know where you've been or where you're going. I don't know if you're here by choice or coercion. But let me tell you, you're not here by mistake."

Will shifted in his seat and picked a piece of lint from his pants. He was definitely not here by choice. Sneaking a look at his phone, he checked again for a call or text from Cordelia. But there was no response.

"Christ appeared after 400 years of silence," the preacher continued. "After doling out miracles and promises and prophecies, God went mute for centuries. Can you imagine how empty that silence must've been?"

Will closed his eyes, immediately drawn back to a dark, dirty holding cell. Yes, he knew the absence of conversation. The utter lack of human connection. The punishing loneliness of isolation, knowing nobody knew where you were or that you were even alive. He'd drawn breath, but no longer existed.

"Tonight, your North Star is here," the pastor said. "The Lord is just a conversation away. You can put down your suitcase. You don't have to run anymore. You don't have to take another step or figure out your next direction. Perhaps you're right where you're supposed to be."

Alex touched his burning candle wick to Will's, and he watched it spark to life.

The lights went off, and Miss Frannie returned to the stage and softly sang "O Holy Night" while candle after candle illuminated the room.

"A thrill of hope, the weary world rejoices. For yonder breaks, a new and glorious morn. Fall. . .on your knees. Oh, hear, the angel voices. . ."

Will grabbed his coat and stood, excusing himself as he stepped over feet and bumped his way out the row. "Pardon me. Sorry. Excuse me."

"Will?" he heard his sister call.

But he kept walking. Down the long aisle.

And out the door.

CHAPTER TWENTY-THREE

S NOW CRUNCHED BENEATH Will's feet as he walked, and he reveled in the hush of the night, the scent of frozen precipitation, and the rattle of the stiff, frozen tree limbs. He hadn't seen a good snow in years, and he lifted his face to the sky, letting the flakes fall on his skin as if they could wash away all the grime, the darkness, the loss.

Will missed Cordelia. And Isaiah. He didn't want to spend the holiday without them. He'd apologize. He'd—

Whack!

A snowball hit him between the shoulder blades.

Turning on his heel, Will surveyed the landscape.

Whack!

Another torpedoed right to his face.

His brother Alex stepped out from behind a church sign that read *Grace Is In This Place*, his arm poised for another round.

"What are you doing?" Will asked. "Can't you even wait till we get home?"

"Nope." He lobbed another, and it exploded against Will's coat.

Will knew that grim face, and his brother wasn't playing around. "Have it your way. But you don't have your NFL throwing arm anymore." He bent down, packed snow into a ball, then zinged his own, smiling when it hit its target. "Sorry if I messed up that politician's hair."

"You've messed up, all right." Alex threw two in a row, one dinging Will in the knee. "You chased off the woman who loves you, you broke our mother's heart, and you won't even return my calls."

"Cordelia isn't in love with me, and I've been busy." He threw a strike then ducked behind a Cadillac.

"Yeah, busy running." His brother dove for cover next to a truck with antlers sticking from the grill. "I heard what Cordelia told you."

"So?" Where was Alex now?

"*So*," Alex called, "how many people are you gonna hurt before you deal with your own crap?"

Will crushed the snowball in his hands and had to start again. "You have no idea what you're talking about."

"That's where you're wrong."

Will shot off a round of four good ones before lowering back to his spot. "Yeah? I seriously doubt that."

"You'll never know what I went through when I thought you were dead—the hell this entire family walked through." Alex's voice got louder and closer. "You're my twin. I lost part of myself when you were gone. And don't even get me started on Finley. She's still in therapy."

Nobody had told him all this. "Why?"

"Because you were *dead,* you moron." Alex pegged Will with a snowball right to the heart, stalking toward him. "Part of us died that day of the bomb. And then we miraculously get you back, and all we see from you is a couple of visits and the rare phone call."

The heavens opened, and more snow tumbled from the depths, as if God had opened a feather pillow and shook it over creation.

"Talk to me, Will." Alex dropped his remaining ammunition and gave his brother a sturdy shove. "Say something."

"What do you *want* me to say?" Will pushed him even harder. "What do any of you want from me?"

"We want you back."

"You think I don't want my old life back?"

"No. I don't think you do. I think you're punishing yourself for what happened, as if wasting your own life will be atonement for those kids."

"Those kids had names. Families. Futures."

"I know."

Will's voice rasped rough and jagged. "I don't know how to make it right, Alex."

"You can't. Because it's not your fault. And it's not your responsibility to make amends. You want to do right by those kids? Then start living. That pastor in there is right. It's time to stop running. You can write that book or not. You can go get yourself spray tanned and work that morning show or not. But you're not hurting this family any more. I've got another baby coming, and I'm completely freaked about it, and where is my brother? Not at the other end of the phone, that's for sure. Not at my mother's house for Sunday dinner so we can talk football and college funds and which way a diaper goes. I'm sorry for what happened. For the love of God, I'm sorry. But you're not honoring those kids by being a dead-man-walking."

"I'm not. I'm—"

"You are. Do you have any idea how much counseling we've all had the last few years? I'm so in touch with my feelings, I worry I'll start writing poetry and watching Hallmark."

"What's your point?"

"The point is, now it's your turn. You do the counseling and you do the work. It sucks to hurt. It sucks to lose people you love, people who depended on you. I don't know why it happened, Will. Evil's out there, and it won that day, but it's up to you whether it continues to keep that chokehold on your life. Hear me when I say this—you're not responsible for the loss of lives. You braved war-like conditions and set up a school. You did it at a risk to your own life, and one day the enemy stepped in. The best thing you could do to share the memory of those kids is to carry on. To live a life of purpose. To find happiness."

Tears blurred Will's vision as he shook his head, his cheeks stinging in the wet cold. "I really don't want that stupid morning show job. I can't do perky."

"Then go back to hard news and do what you do best. Report from the trenches, uncover political scandals, and dodge new bombs. You loved that death-defying stuff."

Will ran a hand over his weary face. "Every time I think about it, I get nauseous. It's like climbing back onto a plane after surviving a 30,000 foot crash."

"You've never been a quitter," his brother said. "So you ease into it. Nobody said you had to go streaking naked through Syria with a video camera and a death wish. Report the truth, be a voice once again for the voiceless. That would make those kids proud. Celebrate their memory by beginning again."

"I feel so guilty even trying."

Alex's hand fell heavy on Will's snow-covered shoulder. "If only you had a brother to lean on."

"I don't need help. I—"

"Yeah, you do. And I can walk you through some of this therapy crap. If I can endure it, you can too."

"You sound like you'd almost enjoy that."

His upper lip rose in disdain. "One counselor made me do this sand table thing. It was nuts. I might've walked out of that one and told her she could kiss my fat championship ring."

Cordelia's words swirled like mist in Will's head. *"I care. The people who love you and want to know your story care. . ."*

It felt like he was standing at the shoreline of the Pacific, and he needed to swim to the other side. Moving on seemed insurmountable, impossible, and beyond his ability. But maybe this moment was his North Star, his sign to move in a new direction, one he had thought unimaginable.

After some time, Alex cleared his throat. "As long as you're adding things to your Life Revival To-Do List, you might want to go get your girl back. We liked her. Right now, we even like her better than you." He waved a conjuring hand. "So do something about that."

Yeah, about that. As long as Will was disappointing people, he might as well add another log to the fire. "Cordelia was just pretending to be my girlfriend to get you guys off my back."

"I know."

Will's gaze locked on his brother. "How?"

"That might be another area in which I highly relate. But that's a story for another time."

"I don't know if Cordelia will take me back."

"Just say some pretty stuff. I'll coach you. I have to get myself out of the dog house all the time. Do you have flowers? Some Starbucks gift cards? Access to quality nachos?"

His limbs beginning to shiver, Will smiled. "Are you gonna help me get her back the way you helped me get Sarah Jennings in tenth grade?"

"I'm happily married, so I promise not to make-out with this one and steal her the night before Homecoming." The smile left Alex's wind-blown face. "I've missed you, Will."

His throat tight with emotion, Will could only nod.

Alex threw his arms around his twin in a bone-crushing hug. "I love you, brother."

Will hugged him back, words far out of reach. This was his family, his best friend.

You're right where you're supposed to be, the pastor had said.

Will Sinclair prayed he was right. "I'll catch you later, okay?" He zipped his coat as he took a step back.

"Are we gonna see you in the morning? Mom and Finley are counting on it."

The idea didn't sound so smothering right now. "I'll be there. But I've got a stop to make first."

Alex gave him one last measured look, then seeming to decide Will was no longer a flight risk, headed back inside.

Leaving Will alone.

Finding some gloves in his pockets, Will slipped them on and slowly made his way to the back of the church to a small holiday display Cordelia had shown him. Though it wasn't her design, and far from it, it drew Will all the same.

With frozen, wet feet, he sloshed through the accumulating snow, ignoring the sleet that peppered his face. The flakes blanketed the roof of the church, the cars, and Will's clothes, but seemed to fly right off the cheap, plastic manger scene before him.

Mary stood in a blue dress, her face faded from years of service at the manger. Joseph flanked her side, and Will wondered if he used to look proud and maybe a little awe-struck. Or perhaps like Alex, Joseph had been knocked sideways with fear and wondering about college funds. But in the manger, with fresh hay that stuck out in every direction, was the baby Jesus. The destination of the Wise Men. The pursuit of the shepherds. The one who the Christmas fuss was all about.

All those sojourners had ceased their walking. Knowing they had arrived.

The words of Cordelia haunted him.

The insights of the pastor shook him.

The accusations from Alex absolutely leveled him.

Without care for time or place, weather or good sense, Will dropped to his knees before the plastic infant, bowed his head, and let the tears come.

Not once had he ever cried for the pain to his body from the explosion. Will had never wept for his captivity. And his soul had yet to allow him to grieve for the students who'd perished when evil detonated so many lives.

But now, as the snow fell like a soft balm on his skin, Will cried. He saw every child from that school. Held their faces in his mind's eye.

Imagined them laughing, playing, and . . .waving goodbye.

"*I care,*" Cordelia had said. "*The people who love you and want to know your story care.*"

Will didn't know when, but one day he'd tell the children's story. He'd do it right and he'd do it well.

He would give a voice back to those who could no longer speak.

And in the meantime, Will decided that Alex might be right. Maybe the best way to honor the children they'd lost was to go live the fire out of his. To spend each day truly alive, pursuing what mattered most. He prayed for the strength to see that promise through. It was easier said than done, but maybe if he tried taking the first step, the rest would come.

After a few more moments with the plastic, holy family, Will dusted off his wet knees and stood. He walked back to the parking lot, his lights flashing as he unlocked the car.

The sound of the choir drifted on a breeze, and he paused to give it a final listen.

When the last note had been sung, Will hoped the words stayed etched on his heart forever.

He got in his car and drove away. Humming as he left.

A thrill of hope, the weary world rejoices. For yonder breaks, a new and glorious morn.

Fall. . .on your knees.

Oh, hear, the angel voices.

CHAPTER TWENTY-FOUR

A T SIX A.M. Christmas morning, Cordelia opened her door to Santa Claus.

He stood on her front porch, one hand adjusting the pillow beneath his velvet coat, the other holding onto his red hat fighting against the wind. "Will Sinclair, what exactly are you doing?"

"Taking you to the Masons." His pillow fell at his booted feet. "Do you happen to have a girdle I could borrow?"

"Fresh out of those." She tightened the belt on her pink robe and let her eyes wander the sight before her. "Did you run out of clean clothes and mob Santa?" There'd be no getting off the naughty list for that one.

Will pulled down his voluptuous white beard. "The roads are pure ice, and you're not getting out in that tiny car of yours for days. The way I see it, unless the town's one single snow plow picks you up, me and my trusty Chevy steed are your only option to deliver Christmas to the Mason family. Now do you want to take them your gifts or not?"

She eyed the mountain of packages in the back of the truck idling in her driveway, most of which looked like they'd encountered a rumble with wrapping paper, got tag-teamed by packing tape, then totally TKO'd. "What is all that back there?"

"Some food. Clothes. Toys. Lots of toys."

"Did that come with the stolen truck?"

He plucked a mini candy cane from his pocket, removed the wrapper in one swipe, and stuck it between his lips. "I didn't steal it, and there isn't a naked Santa running around town. You and Isaiah have five minutes to get ready and meet me back out here."

Cordelia didn't know what to make of this, but her questions would have to wait. Wrapping her robe tighter around her, she ran back into the house, threw on some clothes, gathered Isaiah, overpacked his diaper bag in case they landed in a ditch and became a Lifetime movie of survival, and grabbed her sacks of presents like she was Mrs. Claus.

Fifteen minutes and one downed bottle of formula later, Isaiah sat in his car seat behind Will and Cordelia, happily sucking on a pacifier as Will eased the truck onto the road.

Christmas music played on the radio as they crept along, finally making it to the edge of town where the pavement ran out and gave way to dirt. As far as the eye could see it was white, with the sky still spitting flurries like a glorious encore.

Cordelia didn't know what to think of Christmas Day Will, so she kept her jumble of thoughts to herself. Meanwhile, Will and Isaiah didn't seem to find any trouble having a conversation. The baby babbled and Will responded as if Isaiah made perfect sense.

"Isaiah really knows his football stats." Will flicked on the windshield wipers. "He's putting money on the Patriots going to the Super Bowl, while I'm still leaning towards the Chiefs."

"Isaiah isn't into competitive sports," she said. "He finds it boorish and a waste of financial resources."

"Not five minutes ago, the boy bet me a pack of wipes his team would go all the way."

Cordelia grabbed the handle over her head as the truck slid a few feet before Will steered it back into the ruts on the road. "Do you know how to drive this thing?"

He gave her a quick side-eye and smiled. "Relax. We have four-wheel drive on this baby. And you look cute this morning, by the way."

She noticed he hadn't answered her question of knowing how to operate said four-wheel drive. "I have formula all over my sweatshirt, pureed banana in my hair, and I just realized I'm wearing two different shoes." Maybe Will woke up with a fever. "Are you ill?"

"Nope." The grin returned. "And a Merry Christmas to you too."

Now who was the Grinch? "Merry Christmas," she said begrudgingly. Still, this was all strangely Dickensian. "Did the ghosts of Christmas visit you last night, by chance?"

"They did not."

Was that smile now accompanied by a twinkle in his eye? Yep, there was some definite twinkling going on. "Did you hit your head? Pour vodka over your Cheerios? Help me out here, Will."

He checked his GPS and maneuvered onto another snow-packed road. "Let's make our delivery, then we'll talk." Will took one hand off the steering wheel and rested it on her gloved fingers. "And we will talk, Cordelia."

She'd heard that before.

A group of trailers came into view, and after three attempts, Will inched the truck up the inclined driveway of a doublewide, whose lone Christmas tree shone in the front window. Smoke puffed from a chimney as two young faces peeped from behind curtains.

"We've been spotted." Will hopped out of the truck and came around to Cordelia's door. "Easy on the ice."

She slipped a coat on Isaiah, threw a hood over his head, then looped one arm around Will's as he led her up the four steps to the door. She felt muscle beneath her hand and knew Santa had certainly been working out.

Balancing like there wasn't half a foot of snow topped with ice, Will ran back to the truck and retrieved multiple loads of bags big enough to stash small automobiles. Out of breath and carrying the final bundle, Will knocked on the door and boomed his best, "Ho, ho, ho!"

From inside came the musical noise of children squealing and giggling. "Santa!" Cordelia heard one say. "Santa found us!"

Steve Mason opened the door, his face pinched in confusion and curiosity. "Uh . . .hey."

"Merry Christmas!" Cordelia said. "And look who I found— Santa Claus!"

Four pajama-clad children circled Will with unbridled energy, dragging him inside.

"You're late," John Thomas, the four-year old said. "But we forgive you."

Betsy, the seven year old boss, inched closer to one of the giant bags. "Uncle Steve said you'd stopped by once already, but we already opened those gifts. Are you telling me you brought more?"

Will thoughtfully stroked his fake mustache. "Have you been good this year?"

She clasped her hands in glee. "I have!" She elbowed her older brother, Max. "He's probably on your bad list."

Slipping his hands into his red coat, Will extracted a roll of paper that unfurled and pooled on the floor. "Let's see here, Madewells, Makenzies . . .Ah, yes, here are the Masons." He held the list closer to his face. "Herbert, Donnie, Niles, and Mildred?"

"That's not us!" Riley cried.

"Oh, wrong Masons. Do you know a John Thomas, Max, Betsy, and Riley?"

"Yes!" Max pumped his fist toward the ceiling. "Made it!"

"It's us!" Betsy grabbed two of her brothers and kissed them both. "It's us!"

"Then I guess these gifts from the North Pole are yours." Will extended a hand toward the bags, and the kids tore into them with savage enthusiasm.

"A bike!"

"I got a talking doll!"

"Does this airplane really fly?"

John Thomas backed away from the melee, his head bowed. "What about our brother? Is Isaiah on your good list too?"

Cordelia's heart ballooned in her chest, and she ruffled the boy's red hair. "I'm certain I saw it, sweetie."

Will pretended to consult his list once more. "Well, of course. Right here. How could I miss that?"

Visible relief softened John Thomas's face. "I didn't want him to be left out."

"What about our uncle?" Betsy withdrew her head from a bag and propped a hand on her hip. "He should get something. Everyone needs Christmas."

Will caught Cordelia's eye. "Yes, they do." He pointed to a gold bag. "Lots of stuff in there for someone named Steve Mason."

"That's him!" John Thomas shouted.

Half an hour later, the children said a reluctant goodbye to Santa and kissed Isaiah goodbye.

Steve followed them down the icy steps, wearing his new coat. "Thank you," he said as they neared the truck. "Those kids have been through a nightmare this year, and for a morning, you made them think goodness was possible again."

"That's not quite right." Will held baby Isaiah to his chest. "They get that message from you every day."

Cordelia nodded. "You're their hero, Mr. Mason."

"Naw, not me."

"Yes, you are." Cordelia took Will's hand in hers. "Changing a child's life, making the world a better place for them. That's what living is all about." She squeezed the fingers entwined with hers. "Love is the greatest gift you could give."

Steve Mason sniffed and his lips twitched. "I'll be adopting them, you know. I don't know how we'll make it, but I can't let them go."

"I'm so glad to hear that," Cordelia said. "I'll help in any way I can."

John Thomas materialized from behind his uncle's legs. "What about my brother? Who's going to adopt Isaiah?"

Cordelia stooped down till she was eye level with the child.

"I promise you he'll be taken care of."

"So are you gonna—"

"We better get back inside." Steve swiped at his eyes. "God bless you both."

"And you as well," Will said. "We'll be in touch."

Mr. Mason walked back in, and the happy clatter permeated the walls of the home and slipped into the winter air.

Cordelia stood on tiptoe and kissed Will's cheek, his beard tickling her nose. "Thank you."

Eyes that held a little less pain, a little more light looked back at her. "No, Cordelia. Thank you."

"Can we make one more stop?"

He opened her car door and helped her inside. "My sleigh is at your command."

CHAPTER TWENTY-FIVE

"Y OU SURE ABOUT this?" Will tapped the brakes as the truck rolled to a stop in front of a familiar house.

Cordelia blew out a breath, ruffling her bangs. "No, but it wouldn't be Christmas without a door slammed in my face."

He squeezed her cold hand. "We probably need to work on some new traditions."

Cordelia had that confused look on her face, but Will just smiled and helped her get the baby bundled like a snow bunny once again. The three of them trekked up the sidewalk to Cordelia's mother's home.

They didn't even have to knock.

"Get in here, for crying out loud." Jane Daring held open the door, her hair a wild rumpus. "Are you trying to freeze that poor baby?"

"He's fine. A little fresh air is good for the sinuses." Cordelia handed her mom a green-striped box. "Merry Christmas."

"I don't want that."

"Yeah, you do," Cordelia said. "Open it and enjoy it, you grouch."

Her mother sat on the edge of the couch, grumbling about bossy daughters. "It's a tablet. What am I supposed to do with this?"

"Overload me with gratitude?"

Her mom eased it from the box. "What else?"

"Read, play Solitaire, meet strange men in conspiracy theory chatrooms."

Jane Daring almost smiled. "I can probably manage at least one of those."

"Oh, one more thing," Cordelia said. "This time next year I'm going be a mother. Officially."

Mrs. Daring lifted a shotgun brow. "You pregnant?"

"No. I'm adopting Isaiah." From the corner of her eye, she caught Will's doubletake of surprise.

"Who's Isaiah?" her mother asked.

"The other kid we left in the car." Cordelia rolled her brown eyes. "Don't act like you don't know."

"Huh." Mrs. Daring's gaze traveled to the baby sleeping in the carrier that hung from Will's arm. "So I'm gonna be a grandma."

"Yeah," Cordelia said. "So you know what you're gonna do next Christmas?"

"Buy another deadbolt for the door?"

"You're going to get that baby a present. And you're coming over to my house for Christmas dinner."

Mrs. Daring picked at the glittery bow. "We'll see." She pointed a finger at Will. "Is he going to be there?"

"Yes." He answered for Cordelia. "I'll be there."

"Huh," said Cordelia, echoing her mother.

Jane stood up and gave the baby a soft pat on the head. "You two get on out of here. Watch the roads and don't get frisky in the truck."

Cordelia followed Will to the door, pausing as her mother hollered one more time. "Cordelia Joy!"

"Yes?"

"I was cleaning out some stuff in the attic last week." She let that miracle statement have a moment all to itself. "And I found something you might want to see." Her mother's eyes focused on a spot over their heads and over the door.

Will looked up.

And there hanging over them was a yellowed mistletoe, twisting in the blow of the heat vent.

"I better go plug this gadget in." Her mother clutched her tablet to her chest. "Probably has lots of instructions I need to read. In the kitchen."

She left them standing there in the entry, a woman wide-eyed with hesitation, and a grinning Will, holding Isaiah like a football in his arm.

It wasn't easy to kiss a woman while holding a baby, but a man could overcome. Will leaned down, his lips dipping toward Cordelia.

"Hold it right there, buster." She halted him with a hand to his Santa chest. "Explain yourself."

"I intend to kiss you."

"I see that. Why?"

"Because your mom told us to."

"Not good enough."

Will yanked out the pillow from his shirt and tossed it on the floor. "Because I'm crazy about you, Cordelia Daring. Look, I don't have everything all worked out in my head yet. I know I have a long way to go to move on from what happened in

Afghanistan. And I'm not sure what that whole healing thing's gonna look like. I'm hoping it's not a wacko therapist and some poetry."

"What?"

Will trudged on, afraid if he didn't say this now, he'd never get it all out. "I'm sorry for the things I said yesterday. You're so full of life and just charge right into it, and it knocked me off balance from the moment we met."

"Even if I choose to be an accountant?"

"Even if."

"Well, I don't. Choose that, I mean. I called my boss this morning and . . ." She took a deep breath. "I quit."

His grin widened. "Atta girl."

"I think Daring Designs can make it. And if it doesn't, we can get by for a while. I want to try it, but it's scary."

"Changing course is definitely hard." He fixed Isaiah's hat. "Or so I hear."

"Would you like to follow my example and say no to that morning show?"

"The spray tan life just isn't for me. I had an offer a few weeks ago from network news I'm gonna take. Political correspondent. Part-time until I get my sea legs back under me."

Cordelia preened at that. "Wow, I'm such a good role model." She brushed a hand over Isaiah's little clenched fist. "I hope he remember that fact when he's sixteen."

"You're going to make an incredible mom."

"Thanks. As long as we're talking about things that scare us, that's pretty high on my list too."

"Maybe we can walk through some of these hard things

together."

"What are you saying, Will?"

"I'm saying I'd like to ask my fake girlfriend and her son out on a date."

"Oh." She pressed her lips together. "We say yes."

"How would you feel about the occasional dinner in D.C.?"

"I'd love to redecorate that Oval Office."

"I'll call in some connections." He stepped closer and eyed the dangling mistletoe again. "Now about this kiss."

"Wait." Her fingers to his lips stopped him again. "What changed?"

"I had a fight with my brother. He knocked some sense into me." Quite literally.

"What did he say?"

"He said I needed to do whatever I could to get you back."

Cordelia slipped her arms around Will's waist. "I like him. He seems really smart." She tilted her head back. "You may kiss me now." She leaned toward him.

Will shook his head. "Wait."

"Oh, for crying out loud, just kiss already!" her mother hollered.

"I'm afraid there's plenty more charm where that came from," Cordelia whispered.

"Merry Christmas, Mrs. Daring!" Will yelled, then reached for Cordelia's hand and led her outside under the eave as snow whisped and shimmied beyond them. "After one pretend relationship, I want to be sure this is real. No mistletoe required." His free hand came up to cradle her face, and Will lowered his mouth to hers. The weight of two lifetimes lifted from his shoulders and drifted away in the December air. He feathered his lips across her cheek, smiling as Isaiah stirred.

"Let's give this holiday thing a try," Will said, leading a happy Cordelia to the truck. "I vaguely recall the way it goes."

She hopped inside and took the baby. "This will be so fun. First, we take cookies to all the neighbors. Then, we walk up and down the street caroling. Next—"

"Nice try, Daring." He leaned in and kissed her again. "How about we go see my family and make a few new memories?"

"Will there be pie?"

"I can guarantee it."

Her eyes held a promise of so much good. A light where he had seen only dark. Joy where he'd known the prison of grief.

"Then let's go," Cordelia said. "But keep the suit." She patted his now-flat belly and gave him a wink. "It's not every day a girl gets to kiss Santa."

Nearly five years ago Will had wished for an end.

But on this sweet Christmas, in a small creekside town, Will Sinclair had found his beginning.

SPECIAL THANKS

A big thank you to my generous-with-info military advisor, the uber smart Brian Easley. The opening scene is not quite accurate to a hostage recovery, but the errors are intentional and all mine. Brian, thank you for your service to our country, and for helping out a writer who takes your fascinating information and gives it a little twist. With my apologies to our valiant men and women in uniform who don't live the pretty version.

With my appreciation to Erin Valentine, good friend, fellow book nerd, educator in the trenches, queen of all things grammar. Your help and encouragement is a gift, and this book wouldn't be possible without you. Thanks for making it better with your keen eye and editing prowess.

Muchas gracias to Christa Allan, my writing soul sister and cheap counselor. I so appreciate your time and expertise in shaping Will's story to be even better with your gracious red pen. Thank God we met at that conference so many years ago. May we always be bonded with an eye roll.

For my readers, who still contact me about *Save the Date*, and for those who, like me, weren't ready to see the last of the Sinclairs. You're *"like a gold card, Lord."*

ENGAGED IN TROUBLE PREVIEW

Ready for more Sylvie and Frannie? Come on back to Sugar Creek, Arkansas, for *Engaged in Trouble*, book 1 in the *Enchanted Events* series!

Paisley Sutton shot to stardom as a teenage rock sensation, but ten years later that star has fizzled out, just like her bank account. When she unexpectedly inherits her aunt's wedding planning business, Paisley leaves the glamour of Los Angeles for a charming small town in Arkansas. She's got two months to keep Enchanted Events afloat if she wants to sell and rekindle her music career with the profits.

When a Bridezilla's found facedown in her cake, all fingers point to Paisley as the prime murder suspect. This former pop princess will need the help of her gun-toting, ex-CIA grandmother and her handsome neighbor, Beau Hudson, to unravel the mystery and clear her good name.

Love is in the air this wedding season, but before Paisley can help the ladies of Sugar Creek say, "I do," she's got to unveil a killer. Or find herself the next target.

CHAPTER ONE

T HEY SAY HOME is where the heart is.
I say home is where my cheating ex-fiancé is, so I really hadn't ever planned on making a move anywhere near the same time zone as Evan Holbrook.

But then that certified letter came and changed everything.

Sugar Creek, Arkansas, hadn't been home to me since I'd left town just two weeks shy of high school graduation on a plane to Los Angeles, fueled by the promises of a talent agent and my own youthful arrogance. That had been ten years and many failures ago. And at some point, the failure gets so big, you can't fit it all in a suitcase and bring it home. So you stay away, promising to return when the favorable winds shift your direction once again.

Sure, I'd been back to Sugar Creek a few times. Like when I let my fiancé talk me into holding our wedding here for some small-town charm and good press.

How was I to know he intended to practically light that press on fire, using my good name as kindling?

My green eyes now lingered on every familiar sight as I drove through this town I'd avoided. The elementary school where I broke my arm in the third grade, attempting a master-level double Dutch move. The two-story Victorian home with a manicured exterior as uptight as the owner, Mrs. Mary Lee Smith, whose claims to fame included being a descendant of Robert E. Lee and surviving five years of me in her cotillion classes. (She told my momma a Lee never had it so bad.) The vacant field near the VFW where they held the summer fair, and where I stood on a flatbed trailer at the age of ten and sang Beyoncé songs to a corndog-eating crowd and knew I'd found my life's work. Then the Sugar Creek Chapel, a beautiful glass structure that had landed in every bridal magazine as an ideal, quaint wedding location. It had certainly been ideal to me once upon a time.

But then Evan decided to throw some drama into our wedding, leaving me at the altar and bringing shame down on my head, heavy as that ugly veil his momma talked me into wearing. Half the town had been invited to those nuptials. Evan and I had pretty much been the Will and Kate of Sugar Creek. But my prince stopped our ceremony mid-vow, let go of my hand, told me it was over before God and gape-mouthed man, and walked away. The only wedding gift I kept was a chrome toaster—with aspirations of tossing it into Evan's bathwater.

Fed up with the Southern-drawled whispers and speculative looks, I'd hightailed it back to my beloved LA.

Two years later I found myself back in Sugar Creek. Desperation was the only thing that could slip its hold around my neck like a lasso and drag me back. And desperate I was.

Snap out of it and focus on where you're going, I told myself, shoving aside memories and broken dreams, bitter as unripe berries. I sounded like the therapist I could no longer afford.

My car, named Shirley, was an old Camry that was a daily

insult to the Mercedes convertible I'd had to surrender. Shirley was loud and sassy and liked to shimmy at inappropriate moments, but I guess she got me where I wanted to go. Or in this case, where I didn't want to go.

The old car shook with a rusty palsy while I did a loop around the square. The heart beating beneath my cotton T-shirt warned me that Sugar Creek was where people dropped by for a visit and never left, buying themselves the corner lot and the picket-fence dream they hadn't even known they'd wanted. Like many downtowns across this fine country, Sugar Creek had recently begun the process of a restoration, rejuvenating the ghostlike, boarded-up ruins of the past into a bustling community that looked like something straight out of a Norman Rockwell painting. The square and its surrounding streets were dotted with small shops, a few bed-and-breakfasts, a bank that still passed out lollipops to your kids.

"Come on, Shirley. You can do it. Just a few streets more." Perhaps it was my weary imagination, but the car seemed to rally.

A familiar house came into view, a marshmallow-white Queen Anne with a wraparound porch, and a smile lifted my lips.

I might not want to live in Sugar Creek forever, and I might be resentful of why I was there, but nothing compared to finally returning to the sweet, gentle embrace of your beloved grandmother.

Wondering at the cars lining the street, I parked in the driveway of 105 Davis Street, hopped out of Shirley, and ran to the door. Oh, grandmothers. They bake cookies. They play pretend. They tell bedtime stories and sing lullabies and slip you a five-dollar bill when nobody is looking.

And then there's my grandma.

"State your business," came a voice from the shrubs. "Or I activate the home security yard gnomes. They'll shoot pepper spray from their hats and Taser darts straight outta their knickers."

"Stand down, Agent Hot Stuff." I grinned. "It's your beloved granddaughter. I've returned to kiss your wrinkled brow and make your life complete in your golden years before we ship you off to Shady Acres."

Sylvie Sutton, the woman who refused to let me call her *grandma* to her face, stepped from the shadows. "I've paid good money to make sure there are no wrinkles in this brow." She held out her toned arms. "Come here and give us a kiss, Paisley."

I ran into her embrace like our own reenactment of *The Notebook: Grandparents' Edition.* "I've missed you," I said.

"You, too, shug." Sylvie stepped back and took a measured study. "Are you eating? Sleeping? You look a little peaked."

"I look a little broke." And brokenhearted.

"You've come to the right place." Sylvie slipped her arm around my waist and drew me onto the porch. "Come on inside. You're just in time for book club."

Oh, no. The last thing I wanted was to see people and have to make small talk. "I've driven a really long way. I just wanted to see you, then grab the keys to the rent house and crash."

"Uh-huh." Sylvie held open the screen door. "About that rental . . ."

"Look who's finally here!" My cousin Emma appeared in the

foyer, her eyes bright, her hair perfect, and her hands making little claps of delight. She tackled me in an impressive bear hug. "Run," she whispered in her ear. "Run while you can. Aunt Maxine's visiting."

"I heard that." Sylvie escorted us past the formal living room and into what she liked to call her parlor. And if parlor meant a place where coasters weren't required and folks gathered around the giant-screen TV, then parlor it was. "Nobody's leaving. Paisley just got here."

"Hello, sweet pea." My grandmother's sister, Maxine Simmons, scooped me into a hug, her hands patting all over me as if she were airport security. "Tanned and trim. Could you be any more of a Hollywood cliché?" My crazy great-aunt clucked her tongue. "Someone get this girl a burger. She's OD'd on salads and tofu."

"Quit hogging her, Maxine." Frannie Nelson stood, her lips pulled into a smile that could power the streetlights. "Girl, you bring some of those hugs to me."

"Hi, Aunt Frannie."

"You been gone too long." Frannie could speak five languages, but Southern was her dialect of choice. "It's about time you got right with Jesus and came on home."

Frannie and I didn't share DNA, a last name, or even the same skin color. But she was as family as any blood relative of Sylvie's. The two shared a unique bond, one that could be trying in the worst of times, entertaining in the best. The two had recently retired from the CIA, having devoted their entire adult lives to intrigue and espionage. To say retirement was going well was like saying World War II was a little historical hiccup. Both women had been mysteriously recruited into the bureau at the age of seventeen under a top-secret program when women were more likely to take care of a home than take a bullet for their country. Sylvie had married her high school sweetheart two weeks before graduation, given him five children by the age of twenty-five, then left most of the child-rearing to her husband. She knew more about bomb detonations than diapers and more about Middle Eastern spies than spaghetti dinners.

And, as Emma had warned me, Sylvie was spending her newfound free time on helping her grandchildren down the aisle. So far Emma had taken the bait, as she was now engaged to the handsome Sugar Creek mayor. But Sylvie would not get me. No, sirree. You could bet your nukes on that one.

"Welcome to Sexy Book Club," Emma said. "Frannie and Sylvie already have a husband picked out for you."

"I told Paisley all about him," Sylvie said. "Have you given my plan any more thought?"

"No," I said. "I'm still not up for an arranged marriage to an Israeli diplomat."

Sylvie shared a look with Frannie and Maxine. "Some people just have no sense of romance and peacekeeping."

The room held a handful of other women of various ages, each clutching tablets or paperbacks in their laps, and all greeting me with familiar warmth or unbridled curiosity.

"You look like you could use some punch and cookies." Sylvie handed me a plate as I settled onto the couch.

"Thank you." I blew my limp red hair out of my face. My long locks had started out beautifully straight this morning and were now a hot, humid disaster of curls and frizz. "I really can't stay, though."

"What's brought you back home, toots?" Aunt Maxine asked.

"I'm just here for a little while," I said. "Home is in Los Angeles."

"She's inherited her great-aunt's wedding planning business," Sylvie said.

My weird great-aunt Zelda, who'd had no children, had left me and my two siblings all she had. My brother had received money. My younger sister a bunch of stock held in a trust. Me? The woman had strongly disliked me and willed me her dying business. Such was my luck.

I caught my grandmother's eye. "I'm dead on my feet. Can I just get the keys for the rental and—"

"Let's talk about Cordero." Sylvie held up her iPad like a chalice, her voice booming in the room. "Did everyone read the whole book this time?"

Every head nodded.

"You might as well settle in," Emma said from her spot beside me. "Sylvie won't let anything get in the way of book club night. Not even her exhausted granddaughter. I speak from experience."

"What book are you discussing?" I asked.

Sylvie smiled. "*The Cowboy Lassos a Peasant.*"

I blinked.

"This is Sexy Book Club," Sylvie said. "When we retired last year, Frannie and I decided we'd try out some hobbies. So far this is the only one that's stuck."

"We started with some classics," Frannie said. "But we got

bored."

Sylvie nodded. "Lots of big words."

"So we started reading some of those hot romance novels." Frannie lifted her dark brows high. "Woooo-weee."

"Romance novels?" I frowned.

"Or as we like to call them"—Sylvie patted her iPad—"the *unsung* classics."

"Twenty-first century literature at its finest," said Aunt Maxine.

I melted into the couch cushions and stuck a cookie in my mouth.

"Now, let's begin." Sylvie swiped at her tablet. "Does anyone have anything to say about the theme?"

Blank stares from every lady in the room.

"Any poignant symbolism?"

Total silence.

"Okay," Sylvie said. "Any comments about our hero, Cordero?"

All hands shot toward the ceiling.

"Ooh, me!"

"I want to go first!"

"He was dreamy!"

"I'd like to visit *his* prairie!"

"He can rope my doggies anytime!"

As the chatter swelled about this fictional paragon of sexy, I leaned toward my grandma. "I've been driving for two days, and as much as I'd love to stay and hear more about the main character's pecs and kissing techniques, I'm about to fall over from exhaustion. Could I please have the keys to the rent house?"

Sylvie poked an entire cookie in her mouth, eyes wide.

"What are you not telling me?" I asked.

My grandmother chewed thoughtfully, shouted out an amen to something dirty Frannie said, then finally looked at me, her face a little too innocent. "Nothing. Nothing at all. I was just hoping you'd stay a night or two with me. But I know you're tired. You've got a big day tomorrow."

That was an understatement. Tomorrow would change my life. Turn everything around.

"The garage code is the chest and waist measurements of Vladimir Putin's body double."

My head hurt. "Can I just get a key instead?"

"So change in plans. You'll be staying at the house on Bowen Street. It's a bit smaller and has some issues. When Emma gets married and moves out, you can have her rental. It's a bit more deluxe."

Emma chimed in. "We could bunk up. You can help me with wedding preparations."

I'd rather have a unity candle shoved up my nose. "That's sweet, but I don't mind being cramped."

"The wedding's not for another six weeks," Sylvie said. "I told Emma to shack up with her sweetie and swing from the chandelier of sin, but they're not having it."

"How much is rent?" I lifted my cup to her lips.

"Minimal."

"Okay." I stood and stretched my aching back. "I'm waiting for the catch. There's always a catch with you, Sylvie."

"Uh-huh," Frannie said. "That's exactly what I told her

when we got captured in Cairo in '82."

Sylvie ignored this. "No catch. Goodnight, shug." She kissed my cheek, then her lips curved into a curious smile. "Get some rest. You, my dear, are going to need it."

CHAPTER TWO

I PULLED UP to a darkened house and briefly rested my head on the steering wheel in the quiet of the night.

Two months.

I had to stay in this town two months.

There had to be a way around that. To get what I wanted and return to LA before my beloved city had forgotten me. But the terms of the will, something I'd read at least twenty times, stated that I had to keep my great-aunt's business afloat for eight weeks, then I was welcome to sell. The business itself wouldn't be worth a dime, but the old building in the growing downtown area would bring in some much-needed cash.

Yanking a suitcase from the backseat, I slammed the car door shut and heaved the best of my belongings toward a gray two-story with black shutters and enough Victorian personality to charm but not intimidate. Sylvie owned a handful of rent houses in Sugar Creek, and this one boasted two side-by-side front doors. I tried the key she'd finally given me in both doors, but to no avail. Seriously? I just wanted a bed, to slip beneath cool sheets and let my worry-ridden head fall into a fluffy pillow.

Leaving my bags, I walked around the back of the house, using my phone for a flashlight. Crickets chattered and mosquitoes rudely buzzed their welcome in my ear. I tripped on a step to the back deck but climbed on up, only to be faced, yet again, with two doors. The key refused to fit into one lock, but the weathered door on the left opened with no effort at all. I could practically feel the cool, crisp sheets already.

My flashlight illuminated a small kitchen with granite countertops, white cabinets, and a dining set tucked into a nook. The hardwood floor beneath my feet creaked as I stepped into the room and—

A large shadow flickered a millisecond before five hundred pounds of solid bulk slammed into my body and threw me to the ground.

Lightning exploded in my head as it hit the floor, and my scream pierced the air. I kicked and struggled, desperate to get this intruder off me, while panic overrode any rational thought. I'd taken a self-defense class years ago, but I couldn't recall a single move. Still screaming, I thrashed wildly and tried to claw this person's face, but he took my hands captive.

"Get off me!" I yelled. "My husband's in the car! He has a gun!"

The intruder stilled. With one large hand still wrapped around both my wrists, he reached for my dropped phone and shined the light right in my face. My thunderous heartbeat couldn't drown out the loud sigh from the person hovering over me.

"Husband, huh?" a deep voice said. "Maybe we should wait for him."

Oh, geez.

I was pretty sure I knew that voice.

My attacker released my hands and rolled to his feet, the

light revealing one familiar face.

"Beau Hudson." My volume escalated with each word. "What in the name of all that's holy are you doing in *my* house?"

"You're in *my* house, Paisley Sutton." He flicked on the overhead light, illuminating a tableau I would forever call *The Time I Faced Death and Didn't Wet Myself.*

"This is my grandmother's home, and I have the keys to it." I pulled myself up to a seated position, my skull throbbing.

This interloper was the brother of my childhood best friend. His hair was the color of toffee, and those eyes, blue as sea glass. Back in the day, just to look upon him made a girl want to write poetry and compromise every moral she had. None of that had changed. He'd been the hero of the Sugar Creek football team years ago, before picking up his high school diploma and heading off to the Army. He was tall and trim, his body contoured with muscles he clearly still maintained since his military days. I only spoke to his sister about once a year, but she always gave me an update on Beau. I knew he'd come back to Sugar Creek within the last few years, lucky to be alive—yet, as his sister put it, "not quite the same."

Beau had been the older, mature fourteen to my twelve. After sharing a plate of macaroni and fried chicken, we'd kissed at a church social. Then he ran back to school to tell everyone it had been a slobbery disaster.

He took a knee beside me, and I scooted away.

"Let me see your head." His voice was as gruff as the stubble on his face. I'd just been attacked by a lumberjack. "Quit squirming." He reached out a hand and skimmed it over my cheek and temple, his eyes intense on my face. "I could've hurt you."

My skin tingled beneath his touch. "You *did* hurt me."

His hand began an inspective crawl into my hairline. "I mean I could've killed you."

I rubbed my aching shoulder. "I was two seconds away from ruining your life with a well-placed knee to your manly bits, so I don't think so." My pulse had yet to return to normal. I tried to shrug out of Beau's grip, but he wasn't having it. "I'm okay."

Those blue eyes still on mine, Beau's fingers slowly slid through my hair to the back of my head. "Does this hurt?"

"I . . . I think I'll live."

His gaze darkened. "You want to tell me what you're doing in my house?"

"I told you, it's my grandmother's house, and I'm living here for a couple months." Good heavens, his fingers were magic. "So I think I'm the one who should be asking the questions."

"For the love of—" Beau's expression darkened—"*You're* the new neighbor Sylvie was so cagey about."

I frowned, certain I had the right address. "Neighbor?"

"The house is two units. The back door you came in? It's mine. I assume you're living in the other half."

I slapped away his hands and attempted to stand.

"Easy." One strong arm curled around my waist. "We should probably get you to the ER. Have someone look at your head."

I was related to Sylvie. We were used to people suggesting we needed our heads examined. "I'm fine. I just want to get to my side so I can sleep. Apparently Sylvie gave me the wrong keys." Probably on purpose.

"I can get you in there."

"Is this going to involve brute force as well?"

Brow furrowed, Beau gave my form another assessing look before he walked away, a slight limp marring his gait. He returned shortly holding a silver key. "Let's get your luggage."

A few minutes later I stood behind him as he opened the door to my side of the house, carrying three bags as if they were no heavier than my purse.

He took a few steps inside. "Welcome home."

I stood in the doorway, my feet unable to carry me any further.

Welcome home.

This town had been home. Before I got plucked from a high school choir competition to round out a girls' band. Before I traveled the world and lived large. Before life said, "Never mind!" and kicked me off the train of success.

"I hope you're not waiting for me to carry you over the threshold," Beau said, interrupting my maudlin thoughts.

I mustered up a smile. "You'd do anything to cop a feel."

"Paisley?"

"Yes?"

"It's going to be okay."

"Is it?" I couldn't see how.

"Sugar Creek's not such a bad place. You loved it once."

"It's no longer my home."

"We could re-create a certain church picnic—if that would make you feel any more welcome."

"So you can go and tell your friends I'm a bad kisser?"

"Are you saying you want to refresh my memory?"

I laughed, took a deep breath, then stepped inside the living room. I tiredly took in the charming setup. Old wooden floors, gorgeous white moldings, original light fixtures, and a vintage fireplace that had more character than my last few dates combined. It was a lot nicer than the Los Angeles apartment I'd been living in. Minus a tackle from an old flame, probably a lot safer too.

"So, you're moving back." Beau didn't sound any more excited than I was. He had taken a severe disliking to me in our high school years, claiming my wild ways were a bad influence on his sister. And they were.

"It's temporary. I have to keep Sugar Creek Weddings and More afloat for a while, then I'm selling it and heading back to LA."

"And how is the music world treating you?"

Everyone knew the music world had long since spit me out. "Great," I said. "While I'm here, I hope to work on my next Grammy speech in peace and quiet."

He nodded slowly, not even bothering to hide his smile. "So this shop you inherited. Have you seen it lately?"

"No. Is it worse than I think it's gonna be?"

He grinned, a dimple forming in one stubbled cheek. "I'm sure you'll handle it just fine." Beau carried my big suitcase past a dining table with four chairs the color of driftwood. A vase of wildflowers sat in the middle like a little hello. "Master bedroom's back here." He led me down a short hall to a spacious room straight out of a HGTV show.

A giant king-sized bed occupied the center of the bedroom with matching whitewashed lamps on either side. A fluffy comforter covered the bed, a gray throw draping the end. A slipcovered chair sat in the corner with a burlap pillow emblazoned with my last name. Just waiting for me.

"Don't get any ideas." Beau gave the bed a meaningful glance and set down my bag. "I know you want to throw yourself at me tonight, but I'm just not in the mood."

"You haven't changed a bit, have you?"

I watched his smile fade so slightly, and his eyes darkened. "We've all changed, Paisley." He absently rubbed his right leg, as if a memory had pained it. "This town has a way of reminding you pretty often."

CHAPTER THREE

W ITH COFFEE IN one hand, I pulled Shirley into a tight spot on Main Street. Cars circled around the square, jockeying for parking spaces like buzzards searching for prey. What was everyone doing downtown this morning? Was there some event Sylvie forgot to tell me about?

Without bothering to lock the car, I grabbed my purse and coffee and walked the flower-lined sidewalk to Sugar Creek Weddings and More.

Located in a storybook house the color of cotton candy, the little business had held its ground near the square for fifty years. Owned by my great-aunt Zelda, the place was known for putting on some of the worst weddings in the history of the state. If you wanted glam and glitz, you traveled a few towns down the road. If you were okay with sweating through your gown at Sugar Creek First Baptist and drinking watery punch in the basement, Zelda was your gal. She wasn't known for quality, but she was known for her ability to throw a cheap wedding together in days. If a couple had reasons for a hasty, classless production that wasn't even accompanied by some good cake, Great-Aunt Z could fix you right up.

I noticed the sign first.

Enchanted Events.

When had Aunt Zelda changed the name? I guess it was better than Sugar Creek Weddings and More, since everyone in town knew the *more* was the complimentary eau de mothball smell.

The door chimed the same familiar tune as I stepped inside the lobby.

But that brass bell above me was the only thing I recognized.

"Excuse me." A woman sailed past me, carrying three wedding magazines thick as encyclopedias and speaking into her headset. "Yes, we have the governor's vow renewals scheduled for the twenty-fourth, and then *Elegant Weddings* magazine has their photo shoot here on the twenty-fifth. Can you hold? Enchanted Events . . ."

I did a slow turn, wondering if the bump on my head from last night had addled my brain or sent me to some alternate reality. This didn't look anything like Aunt Zelda's shop. Where was the faded orange hotel carpet? The samples of polyester wedding dresses on zombielike mannequins? The lobby chairs that looked like the spoils of a bad dumpster dive? The Merle Haggard tunes on the crackling stereo? The shop had been totally renovated. It looked like . . . a real business. Walls of white shiplap, aged wooden chandeliers, seating areas with plush chairs, dark walnut floors. Workstations flanked the corners with sleek white laptops, where waiting brides-to-be sat and flipped through gleaming photos on iPads.

"I don't understand," I whispered to no one in particular.

A dapper man who could've been Idris Elba's twin stopped beside me. "Is something the matter?"

I blinked my eyes and sniffed the air. "I don't smell mothballs."

"Enchanted Events is now known for more than smelling like granny's attic."

"What's happening here?" I couldn't even find the right questions to ask. "I'm—"

"Paisley Sutton," he supplied.

"Uh-huh. And I'm supposed to be taking ownership of—"

"Sugar Creek Weddings and More. We're now called Enchanted Events."

"And I'm really—"

"Confused and overwhelmed."

"Exactly," I said. "And also—"

"Rudely late."

Not what I was going to say. "I'm here to meet the current manager of"—I waved my hand around—"this. But maybe I'm not in the right place?"

"You're where you're supposed to be. Alice, get us some tea," he yelled over his shoulder. "And you might want to spike one of them."

"This is not my Aunt Zelda's wedding business. Her shop was a musty, dated, relic of a thing that she hung onto for a tax write-off."

"Then she hired me." He stuck out his hand to shake. "Henry Cole."

"I was in Sugar Creek two years ago. I would've noticed someone totally transforming her business."

"I started not too long after your wedding debacle. But we don't have time to revisit your travesties or hear of my miracle-working powers right now. You have at least five brides sitting out there."

I dumbly followed him down a hall, taking in all the hustle and bustle, the charm and class.

"And those are just the ones who could score an appointment. Word of mouth is a powerful thing."

This wasn't word of mouth. This was voodoo. This was sorcery. "Why didn't my family tell me about this?"

He turned a corner. "Sylvie swore us all to secrecy. Said you'd never come back if you knew the shop had gone big-time bridal, given your own nuclear bomb of a wedding."

"My grandmother is right—I want nothing to do weddings. I'm the last person you want making bridal decisions. So I'm just going to go on home and—"

"Not so fast." He stopped in front of a door bearing his name. "You're our boss."

"But I don't want to be." My voice sounded small, whiny.

He slipped into his office and headed toward his desk. "And I don't want to be a devilishly handsome black man who's freakishly good at wedding details and rocking the business world, while simultaneously canceling out any hopes of the female population thinking I'm straight."

"Uh-huh. Sounds like we're both hitting hard times." I fumbled in my purse for my car keys. "So it appears you've got things under control here, and I'd just mess things up. I'm gonna be one of those bosses who lets her employees do what they do best. Nobody likes a micromanager."

"You don't have a choice," Henry said. "I'm quite familiar with the terms of the will. You have to show up to work at least eight hours to get a paycheck while you're here—plus, Lisa's on maternity leave, so we're shorthanded and could use you."

"Is a newborn a good excuse to miss work? You should really be questioning Lisa's loyalty." I felt as if I'd requested a ride on a carousel, yet somehow wound up in the front cart of a roller coaster. This was so not going according to plan. On one hand, when I sold the business, it would clearly bring more money than I expected. But on the other hand, I was going to have to work in this frilly sponge cake of a store. "I have a lot to think about. Permission to take the rest of the day off?"

"Permission denied."

"I'm the boss here!"

"With a house full of employees who need you."

"They have you."

"They . . ." Henry sat in the leather seat behind his desk. "They don't really like me. They've been waiting for you like it's Zelda's second coming. Your great-aunt was the heart of this place, and I'm the brains."

I was supposed to fill in for Zelda's heart? Didn't she know wedding plans made me break out in hives?

"Here's the deal," Henry said. "You need me as much as I need you."

I lowered myself into the seat in front of Henry's desk. I thought of the money required to get back to LA, to invest in my career comeback while not having to worry about rent and shutoff notices. "I'm listening."

"You shadow me, and I show you the ropes. We'll have you cross-train in every department. And you can be the bridge between the employees and myself. Maybe counsel me in areas of . . . sensitivity, humility."

"And what makes you think I know something about that?"

"I'm guessing from your last job as a cruise ship singer you know a thing or two about humility."

"I had unlimited access to the dessert bar on that boat."

"Also our dress code here is a black or gray top, black pants or skirt." With open distaste, he took in my pink stilettos, the turquoise skinny pants, my glittery off-the shoulder Rolling Stones T-shirt with authentic band autographs, and the multiple gold necklaces around my neck.

"I don't wear head-to-toe black, but y'all go ahead."

"It's protocol."

"We'll discuss it later." Like never. I had a closet full of designer and custom-made pieces from my rocker days, and it made this poor girl happy to incorporate my concert clothes into my poor girl daily wear.

"Your first assignment is to help a bride-to-be select her bridesmaids' dresses," Henry said.

I blinked in confusion.

"We're now one-stop wedding planning here. We handle tuxedos, dress selections, music, flowers, venues, catering arrangements, wedding cakes. We work with all the best vendors. Should I go on?"

"Please don't." I felt as queasy as the first few days on that blasted cruise ship. "I know nothing about wedding planning."

"That's not true. Sylvie said you organized your big nuptials all by yourself."

"Let me rephrase that: I have *no interest* in planning weddings."

"If you don't work the business, you don't get to own the

business."

"What difference does it make to you?"

"I know you want to sell when your time is up. And when you do, I want to be first in line. I have big plans for this place, so I'm going to make sure you don't run it into the ground. Here's my proposition for you—I make sure Enchanted Events stays afloat, and you let me buy the business from you for a fair market price."

Not even noon, and I was already wanting to clock out.

"Without me," he said, "this place sinks within a month."

"Okay, fine. Deal. The place is yours when I leave." The sting of someone expecting me to fail was a refrain that never got easier to hear. It would always be a pointed arrow to the heart, even if I *didn't* want this stupid business.

"You won't regret that." He smiled unevenly, as if out of practice. "We've done a few parties and gatherings. It's time to go beyond weddings and offer large-scale event planning. I'll spare you all those proposals, but for now—we do weddings. And you're going to learn every nuance of what we do. I coach you on the business, and you rein me in when I'm a bit—"

"Of a jerk?"

"When I'm a bit insensitive. Ready to get started?"

"Do I have any other choice?"

"No." Henry was not in the mood to be my crying shoulder. "This morning you'll start by walking yourself down the street to Sugar Creek Formals. It opened about a year ago and is already quite renowned in the South for its bridal wear. Our client, Sasha Chandler, is selecting bridesmaid dresses today, and I want you there to advise." He handed me an iPad. "Here's a file with her wedding details. Read it before you go and be fully knowl-edgeable on the event."

Great. I already had homework.

"Oh, and beware," Henry said. "This bride has claws."

"Bad manicure?"

"What I mean is she's a holy tyrant."

"I have absolutely no idea how to run a wedding business." I surged to my feet, suddenly craving another cup of coffee. "But I *was* in the hottest girl band of this decade, and I've met divas that would make you cry." I gave a confident smile. "Compared to pop stars, this bride will be an angel."

OTHER SUGAR CREEK NOVELS

Engaged in Trouble
Royally in Trouble
A Sugar Creek Christmas
Wild Heart Summer

OTHER SINCLAIR NOVELS

Save the Date
There You'll Find Me

ABOUT THE AUTHOR

Award-winning author Jenny B. Jones writes romance, mystery, and YA with sass and Southern charm. Jenny believes in spending her spare hours in meaningful, intellectual pursuits, such as eating ice cream, watching puppy videos, and reading celebrity gossip. She lives in the beautiful state of Arkansas with her family and an evolving collection of rescue animals. She loves bluegrass, a good laugh, and strong tea. Drop Jenny a line at jen@jennybjones.com or visit her at www.jennybjones.com

SOCIAL MEDIA

Instragram: @JennyBJonesAuthor
Twitter: @JenBJones
Facebook: jennybjones
Webpage: www.jennybjones.com

FREE EBOOK OFFER

Get Jenny's newsletter and be the first to know about new releases, book discounts, and giveaways. As a bonus, receive a **FREE** ebook available only to subscribers!

Sign up for Jenny's newsletter at www.jennybjones.com/news